Orphan Park

Lauren Reynolds

To Gail,

~ Lauren
Reynolds

PUBLISH AMERICA

PublishAmerica
Baltimore

ISBN: 978-1-60749-822-3
PUBLISHED BY PUBLISHAMERICA, LLLP
www.publishamerica.com
Baltimore

Printed in the United States of America

To my mom, dad, my sister Leslie, my boyfriend Nick, all my family and friends (you know who you are!), and to myself, for temporarily dumping the television for my laptop.

"Forgive them, for they know not what they do."

—Mamma Jewell

1.

"Forgive them, for they know not what they do," that's what Mamma Jewell used to say. She said that a man named Jesus said it first. She said that he had died and when he came back he lived among us and was unseen. I imagined him to have been floating around us like clouds of Mamma's cigarette smoke. If this was true, he must've floated above our sloppy fast-food dinners in front of our old rabbit eared T.V. set with my little brother Christian and I, as we slammed each other's heads on the piss stained carpet. The ten other littler ones would've been sitting on the couch, snot running down their noses, sniveling, crying, pulling at their clothes like they were raping them. And Mamma, in her big, dirty, purple robe, would've been passed out on her ragged arm-chair with her ceramic coffee mug in one hand, filled with a greasy film of coffee and peach Schnapps swirling dangerously close to the brim.

If he, this man Jesus, had seen all this, I didn't think he should've just gone around forgiving this kind of thing.

Maybe if he's so great and powerful, he needed to put his big strong, invisible arms between my brother an' me and make us want to stop fighting. I thought he needed to tip that grimy ole cup Mamma was always drinking out of and tip it right down into her lap. That would've woken her up! Anyways, I never saw Jesus. I think maybe my brother Christian wanted to tell me to shut up about blaming Jesus and blaming Mamma Jewell and Blaming old Frank (Mamma Jewell's husband) for dying, but he didn't say anything to anybody, ever.

People 'round the neighborhood were always telling me what great folks Mamma and old Frank were, they thought adopting us all was God's will. That was before she got sick with M.S. I wasn't sure what that meant, because no one would tell me and I used to like to think it was because she missed Frank so much. After he died, we got our money in the mail and she was always around and no one went to work. You might think that sounds great, never being alone and all, but really all she did was get on me. I was the oldest after Devon had gone and Crystal had moved into that motel with that "drug peddlin' gangster thug", as momma said.

My name used to be Dylan before Mamma Jewell and old Frank adopted me. But she had it changed to Big Mac, that was her favorite burger, and she didn't see the point of a name like Dylan which, "don't mean nothin' ta no one". Not like my brother Christian's name. Christian was a gift from God, Momma said, that's probably why he didn't say anything, because people who have anything to do with God don't want anything to do with his ruined world, I thought.

She said, "You got real problems Mac, I tell ya. You ain't too smart, you can't put two simple things together. You don't unnerstand consequence, don't notice things that're right in front of you an' most of all, is yo' anger. You'd try'n fight God himself if he came down from heaven right now wantin' ta give you yer salvation!"

"Course I would!" I always said defiantly, "What's that joker bin doin' all my life? If he wanted ta change shit fer me, he coulda done it a long time ago. He'd just messin' with me. Why should I trust him now?"

"Shut yer mouth boy. That's blaspheming," Mamma Jewell would say, emphasizing the "phe" part. But I wasn't scared of her. With her needing her cane and hardly being able to walk, she could barely get out of that chair to get us groceries or change and feed the twins let alone get up to smack me over the head for blas*phe*ming.

Mamma Jewell thought I was stupid, she thought I didn't notice anything, but I could see things like no one else could. It was like the past, present and future all sat like dead kings, in a circle of stone thrones in my head. Every person I had known or would meet, swirled in a tornado of leaves at their feet, while they sat, oblivious, passing the drink and making up stories, stories that were to become my life. Yeah I was angry! I was living in a world of children waiting for God and that Jesus to end their suffering, while some dead old kings had cast for them blueprints of their lives before they'd even been born. I wasn't nearly as stupid as people thought I was.

In fact, there were plenty of things that Mamma Jewell didn't know. When she sent us to the park over the hill next to our house that day, she didn't know a lot of things. For instance, she didn't know about the park. The park was a lot of things. The park was complicated. The park was its own kind of world. A year before Christian was adopted I used to go there every day in the summer.

There were all sorts of different kids there. There were four main playgrounds, the American playground, painted red white and blue. Then there was the prison ground, an old structure that had collapsed on itself, with all the kids inside, at least, all the bad ones, the paint had peeled off the metal, like letters never sent and the swings were wrapped over the bars. There was the playground of the overseer. Which was filled with a bunch of young mindless babies content to do crafts all day on a glitter drenched picnic table overseen by the playground overlord herself—a skinny freckle-faced college girl, Calli something. And finally, there were the savages, a playground of kids who were divided amongst themselves. They wore paint on their faces, ran bare-footed over their playgrounds hot, jagged rocks and would use them and whatever else they could get their hands on, to use as weapons in their constant fighting. There were the teenager guys on the basketball court, with skin as dark as mine, yet still, not black and not white, swooping over the jangling chain hoops like these seagulls I saw as a little kid when my real mom, the one that left me, took me once to the old Coney Island. They flew over the asphalt with the street lights quivering. They were the stars. And since I was almost thirteen, I needed to find a place with them or I wouldn't have a place anywhere. In the past, I walked from playground to playground, following groups and trying to find out why everybody does the things they do.

2.

"O.K.," I told Christian as he pulled on his black lace up converse high tops, "you'll need to know, the park is complicated...". He looked up at me with his heavy black eyes, questioning, so I tried to explain it to him. "Sometimes...people, kids, do things, things that don't really make no sense. You'll see things you won't like. Some things will shock you. You'll wonder why they don't do things differently," I warned him, "but we are just here to watch, to observe. Besides, they'd never listen to you anyways!"

I grabbed him by his wrist and lead him past the corner light. Christian didn't know this, despite how much I tried to tell him, but we were entering a strange new world. He could not possibly know what awaited us over that hill. Silently, but hopefully, Christian's wrist wriggled out of my hand's bracelet and found it again, with his fingers interlacing mine and his small palm coaxing mine awkwardly. I looked down, acknowledging it, I was about to pull away. When an almost thirteen year guy comes to the park holding some boy's hand, people are bound to think you're a pussy or a queer. But I looked down on him, and he looked up at me. I saw his dark wiry hairs matted down on his thick, round black head, skin like mine, not black, not white, but his eyes much darker than mine. His eyes were nearly black and always looked so full, like they wanted to bleed their darkness into anyone who'd look at them. So I decided to let him hold my hand, just this once, I told myself.

The hill, heavy with summer grass loomed ahead of us like the lidded eye of the natural world. We would be over it soon. Soon I would show this strange world to Christian, I could hold it out in front of him, like it was mine, like I could give it to him, and give him all the answers to it. I would feel so proud to do a thing like that, didn't matter if Christian wouldn't ever speak of it to anybody. To show him that new world would have be enough, it wasn't my world to give. I could watch them, I could hear them, even talk to them a little, but that was the extent of my privilege. I would get older, I would grow stronger, my recklessness would shake off, like scars, in time, the kids of the park were younger than me, but they were never going to listen to me, I thought. I felt certain that I would never have a hand in shaping their world.

Sunspots died on the horizon. They cast, from the sky, a brief light on the metal structures on the four corners of the whole, great, wide, park, then fell, like an accidental death, back to down to Earth.

"See Chris," I said, and pointed leftward into the sun, "that's the American playground over there. That's why everything painted only those three colors. The kids there think those colors are better then the other ones. Now, I know you don't talk, but don' you bother lookin' at me with those eyes a' yours, tryin' ta ask me why, cuz' I sure as hell don't know."

And we watched them, some ran up and their red white and blue skyscraper, some huddled underneath the hole filled floor boards under the structure, and waited for the light to fall on them from above. And when I say "above", I don't mean God, all though most of them there said they believed in God, whatever that meant. They never did much, sitting down there and whatever it was they had manifested in their minds, it never left their minds in any way you could see.

"Everyone here on the American playground has equal opportunities for success. If the less fortunate only tried harder, they would be welcome up here," they would say. But, they'd never say what it is that they wanted them to do and every time a plea was brought up from the groundlings, the higher ups just shook their heads.

Christian and I walked in the center of the circle of playgrounds. The space in the middle, this great stretch of field, was a place apart from all the little separate worlds, a greater space, like neutral ground, most of the time...

I saw Christian shudder as he looked away from the sun to the right. He was looking, I know, at the savage playground. They were wild in a way that when you looked at them, you never wanted to look away. You'd hear people talk about "wild eyes", you know, shit like that. But everything about them was wild, except of course the metal structure that grew out of the ground as if it were a weed. The savages melded together when they moved, like one tendril of flame, separate but apart. There were differences, of course in rank among them, but although they'd break apart into separate tribes, constantly, yet even in rage against each other they were one person. Everything about their life was harmonious in a carnage strewn sort of way.

We averted our eyes from the prison playground, but I can tell you what you'd have seen if we hadn't. Nothing was green there, and although everything in the park was contained under the sun, it seems, when you were there, that the sun did not, could not, reach you. It was as if, in the whole bright sky, there was a gray cloud over the prison and those in there could never see around it. It kept them cold and kept their skin gray and lifeless. No earth laid down for them to walk on, nothing but gray pebbles under their feet and oily yellow lights blinking and buzzing out, flickering hopeful, in a sea of gray.

If you were to talk to the guards, they would've said the kids in there were "bad news", or that they had "evil in their blood", as they flogged the bars of their cells with black metal clubs. The guards were always talking about order, and about reigning in the filth of the earth. They would say this dispassionately, without taking notice that the hands clutching their bonds which they would beat. The prisoners moved and grasped the air with the same longing as their captors.

But if you talked to the prisoners, most of them didn't know much, like they had never been in school for more than a few years, or they'd got something missing in their brains. Some of them were smart in the way of someone young and silent which has seen more than it was allowed to speak about. They were mostly poor and always sad. Some, like Mamma, said that they'd found God, that he had rescued them. Others said that God had deserted them. Others said nothing. They waited to die, waited to live, or just waited. Waiting without thought, I've been told, feels like voices are always speaking to you in your head, but you're too scared to answer them. The voices in your head are your only friends, but you're too scared to really listen to their words, so it just becomes a comforting noise.

They sat in separate cells with rock lined floors and sing inside their heads for comfort.

The prisoners were always hoping that they would get visitors from their old lives, from the other playgrounds, those other worlds. But they rarely came, and when they did, for most of them, the visitors never brought the warm feelings and comfort they were hoping for. Usually they only brought sadness, a reminder of the pain they caused by leaving their families, families who were poor, hopeful, longing, and eventually, moving on.

I knew all about this because my brother Devon went to prison. He shot some thug, as Mamma called him, over some girl. But Devon was a thug himself and never wanted to be anything else. He had acted very old last time I saw him in prison. Yet, he was only thirty. We didn't talk about him because Mamma saw him as her failure and she "don't need no one to remind her of her failures", she said. They never left her mind. We didn't go to that place anymore and Devon had become to us, like one of the prison playground kids, waiting each day like a kicked dog missing its' cruel owner. Mamma said she didn't need to go there because she that place had gotten into her head and that she could see the cells and the dirty, once white walls, the sneering of the guards, she saw Devon behind the bars, but when she looked closer, it wasn't him behind those bars at all, it was her.

3.

"C'mon Chris, I see it!" I called, yanking him by the hand and the two of us streaking down the final hill that stood between us and the playground of the overseer. She had unexplainable power, yet seemed docile, gentle, almost silly sometimes. The overseer was a scrawny, strangely pretty, freckle-faced brunette in her early twenties. Somehow, it was an odd comfort to be governed by her. Her name was Calliope, but all her kids called her Calli. She had gentleness in her actions and a quiet voice. In the past, I had tried to get her attention, I told her stories, played chess with her under the tree in the afternoon sun. She tried to be patient, acted sympathetic, but she had no time for loners like me. She had a whole playground to run, kids depended on her. But not me, I drifted in and out of her ruling grounds, and I didn't need her, I told myself. She was polite with me, friendly, but I didn't follow her orders, I came and went as I pleased.

I pulled Christian out from behind me by his elbow and presented him to Calli as if he were a gift.

"Hey, Cal," I pulled at the back of her park issued T-shirt as she mechanically handed out the craft supplies, paper, glue, glitter markers (and in two hours it will be cookies and juice boxes), and nods, turned to smile at me to placate me. She turned with a heavy sigh, and says, "Hi, Mac, who've you got here with you?"

"This, uh, my brother Christian. He don't talk much though. Actually he don't talk at all," I said. Calli smiled. She rushed toward the big, blue metal box, opened the lock and continued to rustle through the rations in the supply cupboard. It stood, like a stubborn, paint-chipped monument, full of throw away treasures.

Christian took a seat at the picnic table, taking paper and crayons without words, dutifully, religiously, he started to draw a picture of our house. I sat on top of the picnic table, "My other brother, Devon, he ain't 'round no more."

"Why is that?" she asked, whimsically, she was busy, but her words were still genuine.

"He went ta prison bout a year ago. 'Bout a year ago round the same time we got Christian over here. Mamma thought Christian would be like a second chance, for alla us she said, but I think he was mainly for her," I explained. She sat down, halfway listening to me and halfway nodding at a little girl who had put a finger full of glue in her mouth while avoiding her macaroni picture.

"She feels like your brother going to prison, that it was her fault?" she asked, sounding concerned.

"Tha's what I just said ain't it?" I babbled, I wasn't being rude, I just couldn't help it if my mouth worked faster than my mind most of the time.

"Isn't it," corrected Calli.

I didn't want to hear anymore of that. I was getting anxious and I didn't want to glue dry noodles shaped like hollow, curly veins to a piece of construction paper. I wasn't part of this silly factory and I wouldn't do what she wanted me to or listen to any more of her talk, repeating back to me things I had just said, like some kind of shrink. I wasn't mad or anything, I just wanted to kick some shit around.

I took my arm and knocked off a stack of board games off the corner of the picnic table. My face was flat, expressionless. I looked up at Calli to see what she would do. She looked up at me, and seemed amused. The chess pieces rolled around in the dirt under the table, mingling with the beads and broken crayons at the children's feet.

"Well, look at that..." she said, quietly, strangely and took a sip of her water bottle. I needed more of a reaction than that. I walked over to the blue metal box and took out the soccer ball. I kicked it a couple of times, slammed the blue gate, and kicked the soccer ball out farther into the field. I ran after it. Calli watched after me for a while, then turned her back and continued helping Christian and the other kids with their macaroni crafts.

"Hey Chris," I said, coming full circle around the playground field and knocking the ball back at Christian's feet, "Wanna play baseball?" I said while I was already pulling the little tykes hollow orange bat and a wiffleball out of the box. He nodded and swang his legs over the side of the table. I ran around the grassy plain, haphazardly flinging the ragged orange mats the park program had the nerve to call bases, into imagined positions all over the field.

"Go in the center!" I called to Christian, "I'm batting first." Dutifully, he picked up the ball and toddled to the center of the field. I took the toy bat in my hands gruffly, as if I was a great, strong man wielding a harpoon that he was about to use on the whale that taunted him all his life, challenging his manhood.

When we first got Christian, it was almost like adopting a puppy. He was quieter than a puppy. Things passed through his eyes as if he were an old man, I knew it when I first saw him. He was a watcher of the world. He was like a quieter, calmer me. Mamma said I had real problems. All the anger that was in me would just fall out of me as soon as it came like a wintry breath. I couldn't be like Christian and keep it all inside, tidal waves moved behind his eyes.

He came to us and I heard the neighbors talking and even when the social worker brought him to our house, I heard her and mamma talking. They were talking about how Christian was like when they found him. He was kept, living under the sink in house the social worker called a tin plated shack. He was born addicted to heroin and his momma never stopped being an addict. When he was given clothes, they were mostly rags. He never went to school and there was no record of him even being born.

He may have lived the same way as I did before Mamma Jewell adopted me. I couldn't remember though, because I wasn't more than two years old. But maybe the anger in me came from way back, before I could remember. Maybe I was forced to live under a sink, shivering, my belly bleeding for food and my eyes peering out from the crack in the cupboard door. I probably saw my mother shooting up, and people crackling with cruel laughter that excluded me laughter of drugs from the late night to the early morning, until the groups of strangers woke up in the afternoon, sore armed, naked and entwined with the sex of other strangers in the cold wake of the day after. Mattresses were laid bare on a cold floor and I was shut away.

I hit the ball after Christian threw it. I hit it as hard and as far as I could. Calli might have seen it and pretended it was something special. She might have even said I had a future in sports, (It was my dream to play basketball with the pros.) And I would pretend that I didn't care to hear her appraisal. But I would smile and look at Christian as if to say, "Look at the power I have! Isn't it amazing? I have the power to make people see me!" And he would know what a hard thing that was to do, and how important.

We had found another world, a world within the other world, Chris and I, the two of us playing baseball. None of the younger kids who toddled around, gluing macaroni could be grouped and organized long enough to follow anything as complex as a game of baseball. You might wonder how playing baseball could work with only two kids. We were used to imagining by then. It was our world then. We could look out at an empty field draped with a gray sky and see dozens of bright eyed eager teammates calling our names, "C'mon Mac, run! Run to second, c'mon, you can do it!" they'd shout.

I had never known what it meant to be a child, I had never really thought of myself as one, but I felt then, running around the tattered old bases, like I had tornados in my legs and innocence in my breath. All I wanted was never to stop, to run from bases to base because I wanted to, outrunning everything that could ever hurt me.

Christian darted straight across the field. He ran at me, his arms outstretched and punched the waffle-ball into the hollow of my back. I whipped around, glared down at him and flattening my palms into something of a wall, I pushed him.

"You tagged me after I already touched the base!" I yelled at him. He looked at me with intensity and shook his head, no.

"Get out of here you cheater!" I yelled, towering over him. He sat on the ground where he had fallen. He didn't flinch or cringe. No emotion registered behind his eyes as he watched me yell at him. I liked that about Christian. He didn't take offense. He let me be exactly what I was.

4.

"What's going on?" said Calli, whirling around to face us at the sound of my yelling. "Mac, what did you do?" I shrugged. I didn't want her to hear my voice brake, or sound like I had regret. I wasn't going to let her make me apologize, that was for damn sure. I didn't want to be accused of being "soft". Soft kids could be bullied into feeling guilty in order to regain the approval they had lost. Surely that would be a sign of weakness. To show weakness would be to admit that you were wrong, that you needed the rules and the bars of their worlds, worlds that I could walk through but would refuse to be a part of. How could I be part of a world I was powerless to change? I would never have let them understand that much of me, to let any of the Calli's and the Mamma Jewell's, Old Frank's, and the people who were like my visions of Christian's momma, none of them, think that they had that much influence over me.

I looked from her to Christian, sitting on the ground still, and swaggered back up the hill that Christian and I had just come down not long before. I wasn't going to apologize. I wasn't going to do what they wanted me to do.

There was something about those boys playing basketball that entranced me to them. They seemed so physical, so raw, like there was nothing more complicated about them than their own hard skins. They swooped above the concrete court like hungry, squawking gulls on an empty, silent beach. They were constantly in motion. I envied that about them, wanted to be one of them. It seemed so easy.

All but one, were tall young black guys in their mid teens. There was one white guy, but he looked like a bleached version of any of the others; tall, lanky with a near scalp buzz cut a long white wife beater shirt revealing the squalls of muscle on his willowy arms and basketball hanging dangerously below his ass. They would stop periodically to reflexively yank up those shiny, breezy shorts. One black kid with a round, bald head and a silver chain clanking on itself, every once and awhile sprayed out in a mesh of cheap metal, free of its position tucked into his T-shirt, flew up, with the dingy once orange,(but now a muted brown color), ball in his hand. He swooped upward forcefully and with effort, in a crescent shape as he dunked the ball in the jangling chain net of the hoop and then landed back on the ground. In my mind he looked like a sloppily dressed, black moon rising over the asphalt.

"Nice one Chris!" cheered the one white kid taking the

pass from the guy apparently named Chris. By this time, I was standing by the trash can next to one of the hoops. I looked down and examined myself, I was skinny, yes, but in an awkward, childish way. I hated the puffy white sneakers I saw on my feet as I looked down at them. They weren't nearly as cool as the black edged Nike shocks on the feet of the older kids which looked gritty, tough and wonderfully primal as far as I was concerned. My light wash jeans buttoned snugly at my waist and cut off too short as I had grown, now exposing a bit of my bare ankles even as I stood. I tried pulling them down at the pockets and resented my hateful child's body for their bad fit.

"Hey, I got a brother named Chris," I said, standing there, watching them.

"Hey, good for you little Urkel!" laughed the one with the round head.

"Don't he look just like Urkel from that one old show, you know...Urkel with them faggot suspenders an' glasses an' shit!" said another who was even taller than the others, almost giraffe-like, with corn rows in his dark hair and baggy, black jean shorts.

"Gimme that ball, an' I bet I could kick yer ass on one ta one," I shouted.

"No way Lil' Urkel!" laughed the white kid, "We don't play no ball with black boys who wannabe white!" he guffawed.

I curled my lips away from my teeth.

"Shut yer mouth...whitey...you you tryin' ta be black,

you wear yer pants under yer ass an' listen ta rap music when yer mamma drives you ta yer white bread fucking school in her fuckin' mini-van an' you think that makes you black! You don' even know what black is!" I screamed.

They continued to laugh. I couldn't understand this. It was like they couldn't hear or understand anything I had said. They just laughed and floated in front of me like a pack of ghosts, with nothing behind their eyes, just laughter and hollow black eye sockets. I knocked over the garbage can next to me. It was bigger than me and it crashed onto the ground, spilling over with Big Gulp cups, fast food bags and other bones of consumption.

"Oh he so mad!" one laughed, I could no longer see any distinction between them.

"Did you lose yer glasses Urkel?" one snickered.

I had, feeling my face, lost my glasses. They had flown off my face when I had knocked over the garbage can and were now laying twisted and askew among the heap of trash. Looking at them, I hardened my face, walked over to the trash. I stepped in to the middle of the pile of garbage and started laughing too. I just started laughing. First, I did it to be a bad ass, I did it to show them that they couldn't make me cry, make me feel weak. But then, once I started, you know it really is contagious!

I kept laughing until I felt like I was alone in a small room, spinning in circles, knowing I would never get out and not caring. I didn't care about the basketball boys' faces as they stared at me. If they were still laughing by then, I couldn't see them, and I knew that my laughter was louder. It was purer because it didn't care who looked on it.

I started running my hands through the trash and although it was cold, and filthy and rough, it felt, to me, warm and soft like sand, make from a million fragile little particles, particles that slipped through your fingers. They were simply waiting, anticipating my touch and succumbing to it.

I started throwing the trash into the air. It fell down over me like summer snow. I began to dance around in circles to the quiet hum of a type of song you can only hear in your head. I can describe it, but unfortunately, would be unable to reproduce it even if I wanted to. I heard an acoustic guitar, a keyboard and what I believe to have been a violin, maybe a cello.

"Hey kid, kid..." I heard from a voice that broke my utopia.

"I said, what the Hell are you doing, kid?" said a grizzle face man in a golf cart. He was wearing a park clean-up suit that looked like something you'd get in prison. His eyes were angry, but mostly they seemed very tired, as though everyday of his life had been a long day.

I noticed one of the kids was out of breath. He must have been the one to run down and get the park guard.

"I was just...uh... I was just, ya' know, foolin' around..." I started.

"Yeah, I know," he replied gruffly, "give them a reason to

make fun of you before they can find one first."

I nodded.

"Yeah, an' you know what? I don't care. You got five seconds to get outta here. I don't care where ya go. You'd just better not be here when I git back or I'm callin' the cops. You hear me?"

I nodded again, and scurried to pick up my glasses. At that point, I didn't know whether to feel ashamed or self-enlightened. I grabbed the warped frame of my glasses. The glass in the lenses was blistered with vein-like cracks. I pushed the lenses out and replaced the empty frames on my dirt streaked face. Surprisingly, I could see a lot better than I ever had before. Suddenly, the mob of kids mamma would've called "hoodlums", no longer looked like a faceless mass of eyeless ghosts. Mostly what I saw was a bunch of scared shitless kids with their pants around their asses, trying their best to comprehend why this weird little "Urkel" of a kid had been dancing and showering himself with garbage and what that meant for them. Of course, in my moment of clarity, I cannot forget to describe the tired man on the golf-cart who wore a janitorial suit. I focused my new, clear seeing eyes on him. He appeared to be scowling at me. Man was he pissed!

"Git outta here I said!" he yelled, climbing out of his golf-cart in what was supposed to be a threatening manner. I started for the next playground.

"Hey! Lil Urkel...," shouted the bald headed kid in the white wife beater at my back, "can I come?"

I wasn't going to deny myself the wonderful unknown that companionship would promise.

I smiled,

"Only if you can run like hell!"

"In this jungle it's important to keep a watchful eye out for predators!" said round head in a funny British accent.

5.

We had a whole forest to walk through before getting to the next playground.

"So, yer name's Chris?" I asked him.

"Nah, well... My folks call me Chris now, but when I was born, they named me JP. Isn' that funny? JP, John Paul Harrison," he smiled walking over a fresh blanket of fallen pinecones and under a canopy of pine trees. The smell of the woods brought a close, wintry feeling into the summer parade. We just kept keeping on, under the summer sun. The hard lines of the pine needles were the wispy lines of sketches it was as though someone had drawn them, drawn them to keep us company and remind us that the summer would end and that there would be winters to come.

"Why'd they change it? I asked.

"Chris was my brother's name. My twin brother's name. When he was three years old, one day when no one was watchin' him, he climbed up this old book shelf in our back room. He probly didn't have a thought in 'is head but climbin' an' climbin'. I dunno if he cared 'bout gettin' to the top, er even if he knew what "the top" was. He just wanted to keep clmbin' on and on forever... But he couldn't. Them shelves came crashin' down on him. He was killed that day.

My mom, she wanted to call me Chris, she said, so that he'd never be forgotten." Then he said under his breath, "No one seemed to care 'bout me, if I'd be forgotten..."

I knew that his worry wasn't without merit. I had also known what it was like to have my identity rewritten for me, rewritten even before it was wholly completed the first time. How many JP's and Dylan were floating around in the world, having been replaced by these other names, other names that turned them into other people, seemingly over night? First, they change your name, it doesn't seem like much, just a label, but then you're given another one, again, one of someone else's making. All traces of the identity we had built on the first name were gone, left only with the rarely unmentioned syllables of the name itself. When a person is adopted, they lose all rights to their initial identity. The name can be changed if the parents want it to be changed, they can buy different clothes if they want you to look in a way that they think would be "more presentable". They can even forbid you to talk about "what happened", meaning what happened before you were given your new name, before you were changed forever.

Mamma Jewell didn't like the name I was given when I came to her. She said it didn't mean anything to her. She didn't like it so she changed it. All in one night, as if it was that simple. I resented it. I resent it still, because it wasn't her choice to make. But orphans like you and me, we aren't given a choice. We become the property of those who govern over us, at least, until we become so angered that we gather the strength to make these choices for ourselves.

It wasn't that I hated Mamma Jewell, I didn't. I had appreciated her and Old Frank, before he died, taking me in. In a guarded way, you could even say that I loved her. Even Chris, or JP, didn't hate his parents for the loss of his brother, although they hadn't been watching him and they hadn't built the bookshelves into the walls as they should have. But they couldn't make him into his brother, even though they tried. But it wasn't their place to change who he was in life and just because he didn't hate them, even because he loved them, if he continued, as if I did, to let them decide for him, he would lose his personhood.

The playground right next to the forest was the prison ground. Like I have said before, the sky over the prison ground was perfectly grey. But, despite the lack of sun it was always hot there. JP nodded towards a short, squat, kid with jet black hair and olive colored skin. He stood, peaceful if not jovial, in his evergreen full piece army suit, on the blue bench overseeing the guards who were overseeing the prisoners.

"Who's he?" JP asked.

"He," I answered, "is Amir."

"It means prince", smiled Amir turning around looking at us as if he had heard our very entry into his kingdom, or he had been expecting us. There was warmth in his strong brown eyes as if he were welcoming old friends back to his home. We had never met, but I had seen him before, when I walked around the playground. His reputation proceeded him of course.

"Welcome, welcome friends!" he bellowed. He had a deep voice for such a small person. It came as if from underground, deep in the earth like a root, an old root, but small, from a large tree.

"Amir, yeah, I heard of you," I told him, sounding cavalier.

"Hey man, what is this place?" JP asked, his head bobbling on his neck like a dashboard ornament as he spoke. He moved as if, without thought and Amir noticed it, was taking us all in. He was smiling, but you could tell he was sizing us up, calculating.

"This place," he said stretching his arms above his head "is your home! Can't you feel it?" and with that he let out a deep, hearty laugh. "Welcome to my country, my homeland, welcome to Babylonia!"

He studied us for awhile again, as if waiting for some kind of gratuitous response. When none came, his thick, diplomatic smile wavered and he started questioning us. He tried to make it seem as though he was talking casually with us, but that was only a guise for his methodical interrogation.

"You both, I see, have dark skin. I take this to mean that you understand what it is like to be branded unworthy. From birth, you see, I was underestimated. I was the dog, the work horse of rich white men. Born without parents, I was an orphan's orphan. I was brought up by other orphans in the foster homes I was raised in. When I was old enough to leave, I spent my days as a dishwasher in a restaurant and nights as a security guard. I went into the army to fight their war, and by the end I hated that I ever thought I was fighting for myself. I didn't know why I was killing for these nameless men, my superiors who beat me, killing for a government to whom I was expendable… To this day I couldn't tell you what that war was really for. I wasn't important enough to ask, or be informed of why, I was only risking my life for it.

I was nothing. I washed the white man's dishes, I held their guns for their wars and none of them ever saw me coming. The time where men like that run my people is over. No one ever expected me to be where I am now. I am the leader of this country. I watch and protect my people now. It is time for the freedom of Babylonia!"

JP sat down on the ground made of dusty rocks, all uniform and gray. I sat down next to where Amir was standing on the bench. Apparently we were both interested in hearing what he would say next.

"How rude of me, please excuse my lack of manners! Of

course you may sit," he beamed.

"Well Amir, this is JP an' I'm Dylan, but everyone calls me Big Mac," I said casually stretching out over the width of the bench. I looked around and saw that there were guards everywhere, with military pants and bulletproof vests, patrolling in circles around the main structure. They each held a gun with a long pointed bayonet on the front. All had expressionless faces, but glanced at Amir periodically to which he looked at them firmly and nodded upward as if in a harsh sign of approval that lacked the jovial smile he had introduced himself to us with.

"Those are my officers. They patrol the people...to make sure they're safe," Amir said.

It was strange that he said that, he was almost trying to explain away the apparent cruelness of the situation. Under the elevated platform where Amir's tower was and below that, the main guard post was equipped with guns and telescopes which at the same height, were almost indistinguishable from each other. The prisoners, otherwise known as his "people" were on the lowest level. He claimed to be protecting them, but they stayed, curled up in fear, living on the ground with the dusty rocks in little cells partitioned by metal bars. They watched in fear as their captors paced the yard.

"Well, 'Big Mac' and JP, where are you from?" he asked.

"We're orphans," said JP.

Amir laughed.

"Of course you are, of course you are! How could anyone

be anything else in this day and age?"

I was furious. JP, or Chris or whatever the hell that bald headed kid called himself wasn't an orphan! Just because his brother got crushed from under some bookcases didn't mean he could call himself an orphan. That was my identity! I didn't want him pretending to have it. But the calmness in his face seemed to say that he felt like this was the most truthful thing he had said in a long time. He believed himself completely.

"*I'm* an orphan," I said defiantly, "I was born to some teenage slut who had got pregnant with me when she was on drugs. I was born addicted an' she kept me under the sink while she had her drug parties, guys comin' in and out, at least, until social services came and took me away and put me up to live with Mamma Jewell who always says "Forgive them for they know not what they do" and her old husband Frank, who died, and she called me Big Mac cuz she didn't see no use in a name like Dylan..." I rambled.

Once I started I couldn't keep myself from going on. OK, so the whole story wasn't mine, more like my story and Christian's combined. But we were the real orphans and I had felt like I needed to outshine JP somehow.

"I like you Dylan," smiled Amir, "you have an interesting way of saying words. You are like our child philosopher. When you ramble, that is the only time you really say anything, Ha! The child philosopher of Babylonia!" and he slapped me on the back with his hard, thick glove of a hand.

I felt pleased to have pleased him. Amir had that sort of affect on people. They would do anything, becoming each other's rivals, just to have his praise fall on them instead of another, just like JP and me. JP looked at me with a scowl.

"Come, I would like to show you my little kingdom," he said embracing my back and gesturing for us to accompany him up the blue see through steps to his palace which served as a shelter and the roof over the poor inmates Amir called his people.

"So wait, like, you live up here man? You stay up here in this castle? An...an like you never go home 'er nothin'?" asked JP, obviously in awe of this small child who claimed to have lived the full life of a grown man and kept to himself in his kingdom of the park, and slept in the tower of a castle, while governing people below without ever speaking to them. The child god reigned like shadow over his soldiers, he praised them with prominent nod, and welcomed newcomers with jovial laugh and punished with the booming silent fury only a frightened child can possess. I would soon learn that it was that laugh, that jovial facade that sealed the deal. Once you had come in to the country of the prison ground, or Babylonia, as he called it, once you had accepted that laugh, and tried to please him, you were done. It was as if you signed an unwritten contract of loyalty to him. And loyalty to man-children like Amir, was the surrendering of all rights to become the orphan children adopted by a tyrannical, militant father. Loyalty was never refusing an order. Everything Amir ordered you to do, he'd say, was for the good, the freedom of Babylonia. Loyalty was taking your life, if it was asked of you. It is true that orphans are worth no more than there is use for them. "Forgive them for they know not what they do," indeed!

He led us up the stairs. Soldiers on the platform moved apart like a sea for him as he passed.

"Please," he said to one of them, "do not insult my new friends here with the ugliness of your faces and these ridiculous weapons! Vacate this area now and let us spend this time together freely. I am in no danger now. I am among my children!" and immediately the soldier nodded and motioned for the others to follow him down to the ground to patrol the underlings, although it was clear they were still his guards and their steadfast loyalty kept them looking up there at us worrying that every second they missed there might have been an assassination attempt made on him. It was also clear that those "ridiculous weapons", as Amir had called them, had been bought and were used at Amir's order and for his protection.

"This is the patrolling dock you see here," said Amir, gesturing with the full length of his arm over the narrow command-platform that led upwards toward his tower. The sides of the ramp had steel rails trimmed extensively with long black sniper rifles which provided telescopic lenses that moved with the eye of whoever was looking through it, a cross shaped target locater. It moved with the person it sought to kill, connecting and moving with them like a detachable soul. It was the unstoppable, self-destructive hand that could only be helplessly watched by the eyes that awaited the deaths they felt coming, as the sniper rifle took its' life over and over again by taking theirs.

"And this, my friends," bellowed Amir, "is my palace!" He extended his arm for us to proceed forward up the stairway to the tower. JP and I looked at each other and walked up with dread and anticipation. The circular tomb of the tower was ornately decorated with dangling chandeliers and gold embossed wall paper. The huge bed was draped with a beautiful cream colored silk canopy. But despite the finery and apparently new furnishings, there was still a cold, dead feeling about that room as if it were designed to be the beautiful catacomb a ruler is buried in so that he could have all his wealth and worldly possessions in the afterlife. There was a sense that Amir had this room built with the intention that never in his life would he occupy another one. A crypt fit for a king.

The elaborate ring that circled the walls was not merely frivolous design. It was a decadent ring of weaponry fenced itself along the perimeter of the tower room like some kind of militant séance circle designed to keep others out or himself safe within its' walls, I don't know. But a floor with guns ranging from machine guns to silencers that seem to sprout out of the carpet like innocent blades of grass is the sort of thing that has stuck in my memory perfectly since that day I saw it.

6.

At that moment, we saw him. A small, scrawny black boy no older than I was, dressed in rags appeared in the narrow door frame. He appeared there with a rifle, a sawed off shotgun face pointed directly at Amir. The boy and the shotgun stared down Amir and Amir stared right back. His face didn't waver. He didn't shown weakness for a moment, just a look of self-righteous outrage. I could almost hear the words screaming in Amir's head,

"How dare you kill me? I am your president! I protect you! I keep you free from those animals! I will not die. I have seen my death. It has been drawn out for me by God. This is not how I die!"

As the boy's bony hand reached, steadfast, for the trigger, a bloom of deep red blossomed from the middle of his dark forehead. He fell to the floor dead. A soldier was visible to us in his absence. He had shot the boy through the head. Furious, Amir kicked the body out of his way.

"Those who do not belong to me should never look upon me and keep their lives," he hissed in disgust at the dead body. After walking over the dead boy he yelled,

"Where are my guards? Where have they gone? Why are they not protecting their president? I'd think they wanted me dead, as they are not here to defend me! Someone has made an attempt on my life! How many of the rest of you want to kill me too? All of you!" He was bellowing in a childlike frenzy at the sober faced guards who would clearly have died for him but in his paranoid rants he spun around, spitting and accusing them all. He felt that he could trust no one.

Amir turned to JP and I and said, "from now on, I make you the first in charge of aid to the president. Rafa," he called to one of the soldiers he had just accused of trying to murder him. "Give them both uniforms and artillery and have them prepare to guard the tower immediately."

I decided then, that as attractive the perspective that this place was the free home for all orphans who came together in freedom and in brotherhood, that this was just another place where "free" things are kept in cages and the ones who aren't trained to fly back to their cages for the sake of their own self-preservation are met with violence. Amir's appealing propositions, attractive offers of power and a place to call home, as well as his smiling eyes and jovial voice were only reserved for those who did not oppose him. For those that did however, this self proclaimed "father" of the lost children that were his people, would not be hesitant to shoot his "children" at the first sign of resistance. His love, if not feigned, was not without a price, a high one at that.

What great kingdom was this? What earthly realm had I fallen into? What was the meaning of a place where fathers killed their children in order to protect them? Why was it not clear to them that he was only trying to protect himself and create an empire in his name? They were free only if they wanted only what he allowed them to have and to do exactly as he told them to do.

As Amir faced away from us to bark more orders at the soldiers, I took my opportunity to lift myself, one short panted leg at a time, over the steel bars that railed the stairway to the tower and hung by my arms trying to drop out of sight. But before I swung my restless legs and let myself drop onto the slide below me, JP looked down and his eyes met with mine. Mine bulged with fear. I shook my head, to say,

"No, don't tell him!"

JP looked anxious but ambivalently so. His eyes darted from mine to the back of Amir's head back to mine again. He seemed to have made up his mind. He nodded at me and then turned forward to face the back of Amir's head again. At that point it didn't matter much to me if he told Amir or not, at least he had afforded me the moment to drop onto the bright yellow slide that reminded me that this was first and foremost, merely a playground for kids to enjoy themselves with, to live.

He was there for Amir when he stopped yelling orders at his lower ranked officers. He was there for him when he spun around again, mad with fear that everyone was against him. And finally, when he was paranoid with grand delusions of power hungry pounding at the prison bars of his very stomach fat with the power his greed had fed him with, he would shoot JP, the boy with parents who still felt like an orphan, the boy who was living his dead brother's life, in the heart this time. It would have been what JP would have wanted. He knew, as I did, that there would never be any real home for orphans like us. The only way we could tell the truth was by lying.

I jumped from the yellow, worn out pit at the bottom of the slide and landed on my sneakered feet in the pile of gray pebbles that made a plume of dust around me as I landed. There was the distinct sound of yelling.

"Damnit!" I cursed under my breath. "Fucking fascist-loving coward! I knew he wouldn't have the guts to keep his mouth shut." I swore at JP. I felt certain that he must have been the one to have alerted them to my escaping since it happened almost immediately after he had seen me. How could I have been so stupid to think I could've trusted that liar, that wannabe, fake? Not that I had a choice, I had to get out of there.

"No!" I heard bellowing above me as I scampered, crouched low to the rocks trying to stay out of sight. I knew the sound of that bellow. It already sounded gut wrenchingly familiar to me like the familiar, disapproving shout of an angry parent.

It was Amir.

"He does not get out of here! He does not get out alive! This is *my* country these are my people! I am the president! I must have order, I must have respect! This is my destiny! Who are you to stand in the way of destiny?" He screamed, looking frantically down from his tower, trying to catch me in his eyesight.

"There, there he is!" shouted a guard who thrust his gun carrying arms at chest level towards another soldier, motioning to get the lot of them going. They ran like a streaming parade down from the structure and the ones on the floor looked for me while running to join their ranks.

"Quick, in here," hissed a woman from a little barred cell under the structure. And suddenly I felt her hands wrap around my leg and pull me under into her tiny hovel. Looking up I could see through the tiny holes in the floor, the furious, pacing footsteps of Amir and kept my head down so he couldn't see my face.

"What are you doing?" I snapped, "They'll see me through the bars!"

She shook her head and using her dusty hands, dug through the pile of rocks on her floor, bent over like a dog she just kept flinging them behind her. And I felt like a landmine was exploding all around me, but I the debris that should have killed me just bounced off me harmlessly. I felt invincible.

I watched her as she dug. I know I should've been more panicky, but somehow I trusted her and trusted that this would all turn out alright in the end. She was beautiful, I thought, at least the parts I could see, flinging those rocks everywhere. She had wild, shoulder length black hair, black, eyes as frenzied as her matted, curled hair and wore a long, baggy black sheath that cover every part of her body up to her neck, ankles and fingertips. But I could still see the subtle, strong, curves of her thin body moving underneath, with the power and prowess of a sinewy race horse.

She stopped digging when she hit what I assumed she was looking for the whole time, a door made of wood and hinged with steel that echoed the steel used on the structure and the bars of the cells themselves. This surprised me. The person who built this place must've known from the beginning that it wasn't going to work out and wanted to have a way to escape the wreckage he had made. Perhaps he had seen the future? Or maybe he always had a feeling of fatality in the back of his mind, that agonizing "what if" feeling. Perhaps he knew that no matter what he built or as far as he had come, there was always a chance that it would result in disaster. Now that was a person who understood the true powerlessness of the world!

"Come on, help me!" she shouted, pulling on the iron ring handle of the door in the floor.

"Oh...uh...yeah," I stammered, realizing I had stopped in the midst of the race for my life to fall into a trance about the beauty of a scrawny, crazy-looking, stranger trying to save me as she flung rocks.

I grabbed the other handle and we both pulled and double doors until they burst free. She jumped down onto a concrete step inside the opening and motioned for me to follow her.

"Where are we going?" I asked, hesitant to follow some strange woman to my death, even an intriguingly pretty one.

"I don't have time to explain now. It is the underground-railroad and it will take us to a better place, that's all I can say right now. We have to get going!"

She pulled the doors closed once we were in the dark entrance way and fastened several tedious metal locks. Fumbling in the dark, she found a lantern and struggling through her massive black robe. She had found some matches and lit it so we could have some light to find our way. Her face seemed to flicker with the light, so bright and strange that it seemed to not exist when it was not illuminated.

"Here, take these," she demanded, and thrust a heavy backpack and a parcel of food into my hands. "We've got to get going," she said again, only much gentler, quiet, almost tired sounding, like the whisper of a lover wearied by love.

We walked a ways in silence through a long, dark, narrow tunnel with gray, gravely walls that worried me as they seemed so much like that belonged to the prison-ground, or "Babylonia" as Amir had called it.

"Who are you?" I asked, "Why are you helping me? I mean, *why* would you want to help me?"

"I?" It has been a long time since anyone has said that word!"

"What do you mean?"

"In Babylonia we refer to ourselves as a 'we', never an 'I'. The identification of an individual is marked only by cell identification numbers. But sometimes in the other land, the one that we are going to, I am called Lyddie. Lyddie Loveless. The place we are going to, they love names, they often give their people the same name, but they say that they are all different from each other, but say also that they are all equal to each other. It is a very strange place, but their kindness and feeling that they are the great unity of the world allow me to take my people there in secret. Either they are blind to the ways of the rest of the world or they feel that it truly is their world, or will be in time. You may have to live in the streets for awhile and are not guaranteed a meal each night unless you appeal to their government to give you wages or go to a soup kitchen... They also have "jobs" where you work for other people who are not the government, but I haven't quite been able to understand that idea yet. But you will not have to worry each day if you will lose your life to the mental state of a big child who completely controls your world."

"This place you're talking about, it's the American playground, isn't it?"

"Yes... I believe so. I have heard it called such...but only in passing. People don't understand me, the way I talk, and I don't stay long enough to have much conversation."

"I can understand you fine," I said, not realizing what an ass I sounded like with my uninhibited, boyish praise. "So, if the American playground is so much safer of a place, why do you come back? ...To Babylonia, I mean."

"I must go back. Always. I must bring people from my country and bring them through the underground-railroad to a place they'll be safe. And I have to go back to get more people and to make it appear that he still has people to control.

The president..."

I cut in, "you mean Amir?"

She seemed taken aback,

"Yes, but we would never refer to him as such. He is a very frightening and powerful man,"

"So I've learned!" I said.

She laughed quietly, "You have not. He is a great child, and an angry one. His moods change faster than the seasons. He'd as soon embrace you as kill you. For Amir, freedom has a great cost, especially as he becomes increasingly more paranoid. He has killed over a thousand of his own people since his election three years ago. I know this first hand. My mother was his second wife..."

"What's wrong, what happened to her? Did he...?"

"Yes. Amir had her killed when he suspected she was turning his other wives against him and plotting his assignation."

"And..." I whispered hesitantly, "was it true?"

"Never! He simply hated her because she bore him only one child...and a girl besides."

"So, Amir, he's your father?"

She gasped, as if offended, "I would never say that word of him!"

"So you're an orphan. That's great," I smiled, "I'm an orphan too."

The girl chuckled softly, but with a cynical demur, "Who isn't?"

"So...going back then, it's your sacrifice? You're willing to sacrifice your life to save people you don't know and will never see again? You're not killing them, Amir is. So why do you have to die too?"

"It is my destiny. I am to be the savior of my people," she proclaimed.

"Oh that's your destiny too is it? What is it with you people? Everyone in that place says they have a destiny, "I'm destined to be the savior of my people"! You can't all have the same destiny! Maybe your people would have a better chance of ever getting free if you all just took the responsibility to free yourselves! Then you can all say you've fulfilled your destinies, instead of all getting killed in the process. This whole thing...it's just, it's ridiculous!"

"You my friend," Lyddie smiled, "sound like an American already! I suspect you'll do quite well for yourself there."

7.

When Lyddie decided it was time to stop for the night she set the lantern on the ground silently.

"What is it? Why'd you stop?" I asked.

"It's getting late, the sun is falling from the horizon," she stated matter-of-factly.

"How can you tell?" I asked "It's pitch black in here."

"My biology tells me."

"Huh?"

"It's called being tired," then she snickered, "haven't you heard of it?"

"Oh, yeah," I snorted, "that I know."

I started rifling through the overstuffed backpack and found a starchy wool blanket, a canteen of water and a big, embroidered pillow appliquéd by hand, that said,

"I had the idea there were two worlds. There was a real world as I called it, a world of wars and boxing clubs and children's homes on back streets, and this real world was a world in which orphans burned orphans...I like the other world in which almost everyone else lived. The imaginary world."

-N.Mailer

"Do you like it?" she asked.

I nodded. "I knew you would. I read it somewhere, sometime during my travels, and I knew you'd like it, so I made it especially for you."

That sentiment had an eeriness that made me shiver, why would she say something like that about someone she had just met? I didn't bother asking her, because I was sure she would mention something abstract about destiny, or God, or the magical, mystical ways of the universe or some such garbage. That destiny stuff, I thought, was complete bull shit. Just another way for people like her and Amir to act superior without be questioned or having to give a real explanation, since they didn't understand it themselves.

So I just shrugged. I could feel my toes pinching and rubbing on the inside of my too small sneakers and had a yearning feeling for food in my stomach and the pinching yearning to piss in my bladder. I was in no mood to argue theology with Lyddie. I was feeling the physical pains and weariness of this world that seemed imaginary.

I was beginning to realize that there had never really been a clear line between them. Sometimes, the strangeness of an imaginary world sometimes keeps on even after you've realized your eyes are open and you know you don't have the control over it as you would if you were living in your head. But can one always control their own imaginary world? When do the people you imagine manifest dreams of there own, taking control of a world that was supposed to be yours? Maybe that was what I was experiencing. I didn't know. Nor can I say with whole and pure honesty that I do now.

"Do you understand?" she asked, leaning forward towards my eyes, as if her destiny had told her that the stupid words she had embroidered into a pillow was supposed to be some mandatory connection between us. She would not let me have a moment to my own separate thoughts.

"I gotta piss. D'ya mind?" I griped, purposefully trying not to make eye contact.

"No. But go over there, no back there, where we're already walked. So we won't be sleeping in it tonight," she snapped coldly.

Sulkily, I trudged over to a dark park of the tunnel where we'd already walked through. I unzipped my pants. The child in me wanted to look back, had painful curiosity that wanted to know if she was looking at me, coveting the first shameful, aroused look onto my unblemished boy's skin. It was excited at the prospect of thinly veiled, bodily want. The adult in me didn't give a damn. It was bored with sex, the tedious, repetitive idea of it, done for hundreds of years and still pitifully seen as taboo. It was desensitized to all feelings of need to want physical pleasure or comfort or warmth. But still...

I think now, that I took her not mainly because of a passionate urge to possess her as the romantic ideal would suggest, but to prove to myself that I could. That somehow, someone like me, a luckless wanderer and watcher of worlds that he would never have or be a lasting part of, could take a hold of destiny, beautiful, wild and black-haired, could intercept it, penetrate it, if only for a moment, and know that I was a part of a greater, all-encompassing world, when by my brief interception, the course of destiny was altered.

I touched her, ran my child's fingers through her hair over her privatized skin, bone white and moon constant. There went my belt-buckle. There went her modest black sheath that promising desirous mysteries, promising fulfillment, revelation, self-actualization and other rich, impractical dreams. I would say these dreams are reserved only for children or those with child-like impulses, but by now I expect that you knew me, the shallow the deep and the unexplainable, much too well for me to lie to you.

There is a way that time stops during a moment you know will replay itself forever in a loop around your head. Maybe not stops as much as permanent slow motion. I'm sure that by now there a playlist or video clip library of some sort reeling mechanically in the sanitarium of my skull. And if you stumbled into by accident, or climbed over the walls of my corneas, you might see it, wander through it like a museum of flat projections, or holographs, holding the most sacred images of my life, that would be fragmented temporarily if you stuck your hand through them, but were no less sacred for that! That night in that foul smelling tunnel, in complete darkness, with practically nothing to eat, and Lyddie, yeah, I would say strangely enough, that it was to become one of the thin-skinned holographs of sacred memories.

In my mind, these vivid, lusty things play like they did in life, only faster and in parts. Her breath was in my ear, hot and wet. Her cold finger-tips roused the long divet of my back which housed my spine just beneath the skin. There, like on a map, was the location of the shadow of her bellybutton in the lamplight's glow. Now, it is just another clip of course, another disjointed photograph on a great repeating reel.

That impulsive act of sex, that possession as a means of diversion or diversion as means of possession, was in the dark. It was at night. It was buried, deep, under ground. It wasn't something either of us would speak of, or even allude to again. But somehow, I think, that those private grunting and sliding of our least resistant bodies, was a strange power struggle between us, violent, fast, hot and pushing, with vivid flashes of firelight, not at all like what you see in the movies. It was a power struggle, yet one with a shared goal.

It was supposed to be my moment of great control, but all I can remember saying was,

"Oh, God, oh godohgodohgod…" and then finally, "Oh!"

Afterward, we lay in a perfect circular swirl made of each other and lonely piles of our clothes, wet with fluids and cold with the punishment of night.

Her head at my feet and my head at hers, she breathed, "This...this was not supposed to happen..."

I smiled, but in the flickering and dwindling light, I'm not sure she saw it,

"I know," I said, letting my eyes close with weariness. And without my knowing it, until I woke up the following morning, Lyddie placed the embroidered pillow under my head as I slept.

8.

In the morning I felt more like my self, jumpy and unsure. I sat up abruptly,

"Shit, oh shit! What happened...wuddid I, we do? How late is it? Is it the next day already? I been gone all night...and Christian... I don't know where Christian is...What'll Mamma Jewell say?" I panicked, and scurried to enlist the help of my long displaced clothing from the heap of our slumber.

And that girl, well, she just sat up slowly and sleepily, clutching the scratchy blanket to her pale, otherwise naked chest, and she laughed, with slowly, with maturity and purpose.

"'Mamma'? Who's mamma? I thought you were an orphan, like me."

"Shuddup will ya'?" I snapped, "I am an orphan. More so then you even. I was adopted, okay? An' this lady,"

"Mamma Jewell?"

"Yes. She's real good to me. Sometimes she says things. Things that I don't understand...but she's not bad, means well really..."

"What does she say, your Mamma Jewell?" asked Lyddie genuinely, without a trace of irony in her voice.

"Says things like, "Forgive them, for they know not what they do," stuff like that."

"I understand that," she said nodding, after thinking fully on the idea.

"You would!" I snorted, but beamed at her, still in early morning darkness.

"But, she's a real good lady, ya know, an' I wouldn't want her ta be so mad at me fer bein' gone the whole night that she had ta...I dunno, disown me or somethin'," my voice quivered. I wanted to sound like a man for Lyddie. I didn't want her to think that she'd made a mistake. I didn't want her to think that I was just some scared shitless little kid with, short pants, short lived excitement and a shaky disposition who could never be able to protect her or understand her destiny that had been told to her by some sacred dream or God or some other with parents of tradition and benevolence, and ancestors of omnipotence and ideology. Orphans like me were weak, they had no roots. I guess there is pride when a woman copulates with you, you feel like such a strong man. It is the body's promise that the strength and wisdom both will become shared. I wanted Lyddie to know that I was like her. My form, my strange child's body, it was a cruel joke. It imprisoned me. There was no way of knowing, by looking at me, that I knew about things like weapons, weapons which were wielded as personal gods in the hands of people like Amir who loved you only if he could make you into another of his great machines that killed, dutifully, in his name. I also knew about people like Lyddie who didn't want to make you anything but safe, but only because it fulfilled the greater purpose in which she would be revered, where everything is planned out for you and therefore lasts forever, and for whom, was the only way for things "mean something". Grown people like Mamma Jewell would never know the worlds that that I passed through, and the understanding I had acquired. I understood that when people are viewed from a distance there is no understanding them.

"Don't worry Changeling," said Lyddie, seeing the anguish in my face and feeling concern, "time passes differently here than it does in the outside world. Here, everything is urgent, and needs to be acted on immediately. That's why our days are much shorter, and also why we are much older than we look. We absorb time like skin absorbs the sun. We have not been alive as long as those like your Mamma Jewell, but we who inhabit the playground have lived more, lived through more, than the adults of your world ever have."

"Then how will I know when I have to go home?" I asked.

She smiled, as if to say that I already knew the answer.

"When you have to go, you'll know. At that time, it will be the only thing for you to do."

I sighed, and sat down next to her, "You talk like a magic 8 ball. 'In time you will know' and 'most definitely this will come true'. You don't say anything specific because you don't really know. You're just guessing like everyone else!"

But she still had that damned, calm, infuriating smile.

"Maybe what you say is true. Maybe I am, 'just guessing' 'like everyone else', but that doesn't mean that it is not true," she said.

"By the way, why did you call me that?" I asked.

"I didn't call you anything," she said. I was furious. She seemed completely unaware that that was a blatant lie.

"Yes you did! You called me 'changeling'. What the hell does that mean?"

Lily looked up at me, confused and hurt, "It's your name," she replied matter-of-factly.

"No. No it's not. My name's Mac, well...I was born Dylan...but it was changed...and now..."

"It's my name for you. I had to wait until I knew you to give you a name. A person cannot name another person just anything that strikes their fancy. They have to wait and discover what that person is more than anything, what they need. A name should be made to fit you, not the other way around. You should be born before the name so that you will never be another person's manifestation."

I had no idea what she was talking about. I figured that must be the sort of thing that girls said, at least, strange, confused girls like Lyddie.

"I think we'd better get going," I said before she had the chance to. It was something that needed to be said. After all, what was the good of this destiny that Lyddie believed in so fiercely, if it was so weak that it could be completely changed by one unplanned act?

After we had greedily consumed of the dried meat and bead from the food parcel and our draining of the last water from the canteen, Lyddie and I continued our long trek down the tunnel's monotonous trail. It was only a matter of time, mere hours, before we reached the end.

As we approached a large wooden door, one similar to the one in the ground that we had climbed into, I paused and placed the backpack I was carrying down on the floor.

"So…I guess this is it?" I said hesitantly. I realized then how frightened I was. So much so that I would have preferred to have stayed in that long dark room with Lily forever, than have ventured out into this new land that was supposed to be so safe and so free. But there I was, dreading it.

Lyddie nodded and I pushed on the big wooden frame, forcing it open. After doing so I was struck with amazement. All around us was a circle, as if suspended in an elaborate web, industry and skyscraper, towering impetuous power and feelings of foreboding hung all around us. It was exciting. I felt that the possibilities were endless. It was almost as gray as the prison ground, except almost in reverse. There, it had been that the sky always seemed gray, but here, here in the American playground, it was the ground, the people and the impressive, colossal buildings which were drab and unappealing. As overwhelming as their power and majesty appeared, they had a generic ugliness to them, unpleasant, as though without the aesthetic of life.

Both similar and not similar in it's ways to the prison ground. There was a large platform-like building around which everything else was positioned. Like with the prison ground, it was a wide platform that lead up to a great pinnacle. I don't know if tower would be the right word, since it lacked all the history and archaic adornments of Amir's tower. In fact, it had a clean, sleek look but over all had a lack of aesthetics that could have identified it as being the product or possession of any individual. Similar to the skyscrapers that surrounded it, there was an element of precision and calculation to it that looked like a number of lesser, far more blemished people had been used to sculpt its perfection.

As I wandered around, looking upwards, practically spinning in circles trying to see all the metal structured glory, that I almost forgot that this place was inhabited by people. Lyddie grabbed my arm,

"Come on Change," she said, as she ran childishly, while she pulled on my sleeve, and tried to drag me to the platform, "we need to introduce you to management! Just wait 'til you see the Machine! He'll tell you everything you need to know...ever! He is a very impressive man."

"What, like the Wizard of Oz? He gonna tell me that all I need ta git home is ta click my heels three times an..."

"I don't know what a 'Wizard of Oz' is, but the Machine

would tell you that the world is your home. And that, if you work hard enough and live by your own rules, one day, everything you want, will be yours. The Machine doesn't believe in destiny either. He says, in his strange, gravely, old voice,

"Now, Lyddie, see here, listen to the old Machine here. The only destiny that exists in this world is the one you make for yerself."

"...And I say, well that just doesn't make any sense, because, if you are the one who has the power to control your own destiny, then there isn't any destiny at all, only a series of choices with no thought or understanding behind them. But the Machine, you'll see, just lets out a big laugh, it's rather frightening the first time you hear it, that comes from way down in his belly, and slaps you on the back. He really doesn't understand that there are places in the world and people that don't live by his rules. He thinks it's because they are uncivilized and do not know the truth. There's no point trying to convince him otherwise...not that he doesn't mean well. He just doesn't want to live in a place where he can't be in control."

I couldn't believe what she was saying. She seemed so taken in by this tall, shiny, powerful place that she had temporarily forgotten about her own self proclaimed mission.

"What about your people, the people of Babylonia? If these people here, they so free and strong, why can't they help you? Can't you tell them what's going on there?

Maybe these people could help those people Amir is keeping prisoners?" I tell her.

Lyddie shook her head.

"You do not understand either. Here, they are free to fight for what they want. They will only fight for something if it benefits them somehow. They feel superior to us, but they will never say it directly, only hint that if we were truly free we would overthrow Amir ourselves."

"That don't make any sense. You even asked this guy 'bout it?"

She smiled that infuriating smile which had as much condescending in it as her prophetic notions of destiny ever did.

"He would never...they would never risk their freedom. You don't know them, Change. It's the way they do things around here."

"What, they way they do things 'round here is by doin' nothin'?"

Lyddie shrugged, "Pretty much. You'd see it that way I think."

"So they free, huh? They real free. Yeah. Sittin' around, doin' what? I'll tell ya what, nothin', that's what! Nothin' but helpin' themselves. They're doin' nothin' so they don't have ta see nothin' that pisses 'em off, so they don't have ta fight for it. If ya don't have ta fight, then ya never have ta lose. So ya can be free, just as long as it don't never bother you that your "freedom" rests on yer decision not ta care 'bout nothin'! Makes sense! Yeah, makes perfect sense! Bunch a' fuckin' idiots!" I ranted. These were the days when I saw only one way to do things. There was the right way, and then there was, well, to use my words back then, "the way of the fuckin' idiots."

But Lyddie was always smarter then me. She knew when words wouldn't fit her cause. I also believed that she knew exactly what everyone would say and do before they did it. Not because of destiny, and not because of divine intervention, or any of that, but, because she watched us, our actions, and saw what we wanted through them. No, I still can't see that either destiny or divine intervention had ever done me much good. To Lyddie, we were all just pawns on the board, she just had to stay quiet long enough to get a good reading of us, to see how we moved. And once she saw how we moved, she knew that we would keep on moving that same way, but like any smart pawn, she couldn't always tell in which direction I would go.

Sure enough, my direction was to the big man himself. Because every functioning playground has a "big man", even when the big man's not really a man at all, but a large child, and even though all functioning playgrounds didn't in fact, function well at all.

I pulled away from her grip and could see his back and I knew at once it was him, The Big Machine. Like Amir, he appeared to be the object of many an attentive ear and had the circle of weaker men all around him, hunched in stature, nodding and clinging to his every word, waiting for approval or a clue of what to do next.

He turned around as I approached him and it definitely seemed as though he had sensed my coming. Unlike Amir however, The Machine was huge in stature. He wore a crisp black fedora and a white, three piece suit that clung to every in of his enormous pot belly, and a pocket watch that burgeoned out of his breast pocket, he looked like a strange mix of Colonel Sanders and the white rabbit from *Alice In Wonderland.* Wispy white hair peaked out from underneath the too tight hat and it matched the wiry pubic beard that pointed out from the knob on the bottom of his face. On anyone else, that "knob" would've been a chin, as it were. But there was something alien-like about this enormous smiling man. It was as though he wasn't real, quite, but wanted to be. He was a creation, ridiculous in appearance and easily malleable in mind. He was fully made up, to suit his creator's purpose. His creator, of course, was no one less that himself.

"What can I do you for, mah friend?" he asked me as I approached him.

"Well, I wanted ta tell you were I just bin' an' ta ask if you an' yer guys here couldn't help…" I was more scared than I intended to be in the presence of such a creation. It was true, he had real presence, and it wasn't just his size. He might not have been genuine, but he seemed to exude more life than anyone on the platform. Like a detailed hologram, he was almost hyper-real, but when you really close you realized that there was no depth to the detailed picture. You could stick your hand right through him.

"Here, why dontcha all sit down now?" He boomed in his cheerful, yet overpoweringly loud voice. He had already pushed me down into the lap of a voluminous black leather couch whose depth and softness consumed me and I thought that I was going to sink down into it forever and it would swallow me whole.

"Weeeelll! If it ain't Lyddie Loveless! Lil' miss Destiny herself! Siddown, siddown mah dear!" He hollered and slapped Lily playfully on the back. She cringed and smiled meekly. It was not her way or the way of the world from which she had come, to be pawed at casually and without thought. For Lyddie, even when touch was not pre-meditated, it still was rich in passion.

He pushed her down on the couch next to me.

"I'm the Machine, if ya ain't heard. An' here in the American playground, as I'm always tellin' miss Lyddie here, where we got a little thing called freedom, we make our own destiny! Everything you want in the world, take it! It's yours!" he boomed again, this time wailing his massive arms in the air like a pair of heavy, impassioned windmills gone awry.

"Yeah, Mistah Machine, I heard a' you alright. I heard you believe in freedom. An' Lily and I, we need ya ta make good on yer word…"

"What word is that son?" he asked.

"Freedom, *Sir*," I said. I did not like that arrogant, ignorant manner in which he called me "son".

"Why, look around ya boy! Have ya ever seen such a

splendid display o industry in yo life? No? I thought not. Well, ah am the Pi-o-neer of industry if ah do say so myself. And ah do!" he laughed again, slapped his knees and rocking back and forth on his haunches, braying like a donkey.

"Ah just love industry, it's the free man's tool I'll tell ya..."

"Tool? I do not understand, tool to do what?" asked Lily looking confused.

"The tool, mah darlin' to sculpt the future with! Opportunities, opportunities for everyone! They rain down on us here, it's like standin' under great Niagra herself! We all have the same opportunities here, you'll soon find out. No one here got no excuse not to make a great man outta himself, shoot, ah did!" Then The Machine looked over his shoulder towards his crowd of cowering minions, one of whom handed him a fat cigar and lit it for him once it was between his thick lips.

"An' how can this be that you can all be free to do whatever it is you want, and yet you claim that everyone is equal? Certainly, if an individual man could have whatever he wanted he wouldn't want to be put on the same level as anyone else. Certainly he'd want to be better.

And what about them over there? Those people sleepin' under your bridges and redeeming your garbage, how come they're down there and you're up here huh? How come then, if, supposedly, "you're all equal? Or have equal opportunity? No one would ever choose to live like that," I sneered, fidgeting to get my rear fully planted in the sinking marshmallow of a couch.

"Huh?"said a dumbstruck Machine, who was beaming at a blushing, sinewy, tall young blond man with horn rimmed glasses who seemed to be blooming at the old mans appraisal. The blond man pushed his glasses up onto the bridge of his nose, trying to look superior but appearing haughty instead.

"Well…" guffawed the blond under his breath, "we're all equal, but some of us are more equal than others." Then his voice grew louder, "Ah'll tell ya why, they're lazy that's why! They don't know wanna work, they don't know what work is, they don't know what they want! And even if they do, they can't take it! An' you wanna know why they can't take what they want?" he was screaming now, leaning forwards, hovering over us glowering. Spittle sprayed from the lips on his reddened, tyrannical face which no longer boasted its good natured appeal.

"Because they're too damn WEAK!"

Lyddie seemed to be used to this type of behavior. After all, Amir was her father and I knew from experience how apt he was to change from good natured, down right jovial even, to raging, and paranoid and violent the very next minute. But still, there was no doubting that even during his best moods he, (and the Machine as well) was always a tyrant. He was a ruler, and the number one necessity of a ruler is control. He fought to get it, and he would spend his life fighting to keep it. He only raged when his control was questioned. There is no rest for men like them.

"Where we, I mean, I come from, Sir, destiny does exist. People cannot control the life in which they are born into," Lyddie said.

Looking at her, his reddened face softened but it was replaced with the diplomatic condescending that one uses to placate a small child, a woman or a dog.

"This is whatcha just don't unnerstand darlin', things ain't any differn't just because you go someplace else. See here, there's one God, a little old man way up there in the clouds, if he's there, if you consent that he's there, it don't matter where you go. Hell, you can go ta Buddhapest fer Chrissake, (they're all heathens there,) an' it'll still be him watchin' over ya. So, what I'm sayin' is that if destiny don't exist here, an' it don't, then it don't exist nowhere else neither," he ended his saccharine-sweet monologue with and irritatingly fake smile.

"When these people are born, they're born in cells, they live in cells. They are watched night and day. If they were ever discovered leaving those cells they would be killed on the spot, or better yet, tortured, not like any torture you've ever known but hung by their skin until the president decides their demons have been exorcised. Then, they are killed. So, with all due respect Sir, if your way is not the way of the world, (and it is not,) and by your own rule forces cannot exist in one part of the world and not in another, then perhaps it is you and your people who are mistaken?" said Lyddie, anger welled up behind her calm façade of a voice.

The Machine sat stupidly and for all his anger could not comprehend Lyddie's challenge to his authority on the subject.

He turned to the blond man who was unwrapping a carton of doughnuts and passing them around to his friends while gnawing rabidly on another sweet already wallowing around in his mouth.

"Do they have nucular weapons over in..." the Machine started to ask him. He turned back to Lily, "What was that place y'all come from again?"

"Babylonia," said Lyddie.

"Yeah, Wilson," said the Machine to the young guy, "do they have nucular weapons over in Babylonia?"

"No Sir," Wilson replied disinterestedly, "they do not."

The Machine looked pleased.

"Good, good to hear!" and then muttering under his breath, " bunch a' uncivilized heathens..." He looked to us again, shaking his head and clicking his tongue, "Real shame, that's a real shame what some people have ta live through..."

"So will you help us then?" I asked.

"Well, you know, we'd love ta son, but we really feel that people should fight there own battles. It's the only way they can really call their victory their own, it's the only way to be free."

"They aren't looking for any victory," I fumed, "they just want to be able to leave their houses without fear of being shot!"

He looked like he'd had just about enough of this conversation and I could see that these people were clearly not going to help Lyddie.

I turned to her and stood up. I extended my arm to help her up,

"C'mon, let's go. These pigs ain't doin'nothin' for us. They don't do nothin' unless it covers their own ass. Freedom. Bullshit. They're 'bout as free as ponies trottin' round a pen. They can git ahead of one another, but they'll never git outta the ring."

Lyddie looked down, I could see that she was blushing. Public displays of emotion seemed to embarrass if not frighten her.

"Yes. I see that it is true...what you say," she whispered to me. Then, she looked up at The Machine, and said, "I must be going anyway, my friend. I hope that this..." she nodded in my direction, "will not effect our...arrangement."

"Well...ugh ha ha," he stuttered, clearing his throat and crossing his thick, suit clad legs, exposing black silk sock and pale, hairy ankles. He wasn't so powerful, I thought. Just another kid, who looked like an old man, who had a spotted liver, worked all his life so he could buy nice suits but now didn't know how to wear them, and who was scared of dying. "Ya mean, bringin' these folks," he said, and gestured towards me, "over from that place ya' come from?"

She nodded.

"'Course, 'course it is darlin'. I don't want y'all to think that we're all a bunch a' heathens now!"

"No," said Lyddie reaching for my hand, "we know you're nothing like us." She spoke curtly and I knew she meant it.

We left him, the great "Machine" who came from nothing to rule the American playground, as the legend goes, who ranted about heathens with bad accents who had no respect for the self made man. As we walked away from them, I turned, and as could have been expected, I saw a pool of his minions, their heads bobbled in fierce agreement like those cheap dolls you stick on the dashboard of your car. They nodded as if on a principle of great importance while one of the men lifted a case of expensive imported beer onto the table, which they all snatched up greedily as another man passed around a bag of hot, fast-food lunches in grease soaked papers. Even though I was starving, I felt as though I hadn't eaten in days, the smell made my stomach churn.

I also saw Wilson, The Machine's head "boy in charge", look away from them. He met my eye, as I watched them while we departed, with a look of longing. As if to say,

"I wonder where they're going? I wonder what adventures will worm their way into their hearts and teach them lessons they'll never forget as long as they live?"

And there was a look of envy, as if every bone in his body wanted him to stop being too scared to stop nodding at every word the Machine said and to follow us on our path wherever we were going. And then bid us goodbye when he came to his own choice of detour.

He wasn't going to do that, though. He was too afraid. But the envy in his eyes begged for courage, excitement, adventure and revelation. That was enough for me to know that there was still some amount of child left in him.

But this story wasn't his, it was mine. And I think he knew that too.

9.

Lyddie pulled me by the hand down to ground level, which found me at her leaving, by way of the wooden door in the ground and the long dark tunnel, to go back to Babylonia and fulfill her destiny. As she opened the heavy double doors and disappeared into the tunnel, part of me wanted to go back with her. Moving back and forth between these crazy worlds was just a game for me. What did I have to loose? If anything, maybe I could help her, find purpose in myself knowing I had risked my life for the freedom of others. And maybe find purpose through the gratitude and eventual love from Lyddie.

But I didn't go with her, I didn't even ask to. Maybe something in me felt that Lyddie herself did have a destiny and her alone, just because she believed so faithfully in it that the great, invisible, swirling forces of the universe gathered themselves into action just for her wanting of it, to make it so. She wanted this so badly that although she called it destiny, going back to save her people had broken the barrier to a greater need, one could even call it choice.

And if she had felt that it was in her destiny for me to come with her, then she would have asked me herself. It would've been what she had wanted. But as it happened, it wasn't.

And that was why, before she turned to walk into the blackness of the tunnel's mouth, she lifted my hand up to her lips. She raised her dark eyes level to mine and looked into me with an understanding smile. In them I could see all of her beautiful insanity. She kissed my hand and I knew she was happy. She had a quest ahead of her, a purpose to her risks and her adventures, a noble cause to die and live for. It gave meaning to everything she did. And of that, I was envious.

Lyddie turned, slipped into the darkness and vanished under the silk skin of the earth. She didn't go quickly, fleeing with violence, afraid of regret, nor did she linger, hanging on past sentiments any longer than was necessary. In that sense, she was a very rational crazy person, never fearful or indulgent. She walked away, straight and confident into the tunnel without hesitation. The door stood, looming in her wake, swinging helplessly from its' hinges, shaking from her forcing through it. Now that was real fate at work.

I could follow her, I thought. No, I wouldn't do that. So I let her go back, back to the tunnel that would lead her to the home that kept her in fear, fear of her tyrannical father and fear for the future of her enslaved people. But she would also be going back to a place in her mind. It was a place that I had temporarily interrupted, her mental place in the sun where everything was understood in grand design, inscribed into the future with the lyrics of the past.

I decided that I would go to the last part of the park that I hadn't yet ventured to. Yes, the last society left at the park was the savage playground. Maybe if I went there I could somehow put all the parts, all the miniature "civilizations" and all the ways and powers they represented together and make sense of this strange, senseless world. They might have been rumored to be inhumane and uncivilized, but at that point I had had enough of so-called humanity and civilization. I thought that maybe the "inhumanity" of fighting to the death tribalism, as "uncivilized" as it may be, might have been the kindest way for people to destroy each other while bidding for power.

Thoughts of the future flooded my head as I looked across the green field that separated the American playground from the savage playground. I thought of Christian, of what he could be thinking and feeling, overwhelmed in place that he couldn't control, affect or change. How would a voiceless orphan fare in a world of success through ownership and belonging? Not well. I knew this because of how similar our situations were. I had always felt that Christian and I were similar. Even though we weren't biological brothers, we were closer. We were closer than biological brothers because we were both orphans who had experienced the same type of life, separately, and then, brought together by chance in the sort of way that was meant for the powerless to come together to change things forever.

I saw pictures of him in my mind as I ran through the strong, high grasses of the warm plains. I felt the flowers buried deep in green weeds rubbed off their powdery essences on my bare ankles. I felt the sweat form in the creases of my forehead and trickle down my shining, brown face like triumphant tears. With my eyes closed and my teeth gritted with power, I felt, with foolish certainty, that if only I could have learned the ways of this last foreign playground I could find my life again. My life, but one with a fate of my own choosing. I would have had Mamma Jewell waiting for me at home, expecting me home as if I were her own, real son. I would have had Lily to make me feel like a man, strong and full of purpose. And I would have Christian to look up to me, so I could guide him, and when we would go to the park, there would be one playground, where everyone moved freely from one side to another observing all others without ownership or brutality. Those were my thoughts of a utopia, yet I knew that, they couldn't exist outside of my head. They haunted me.

In front of me was a great divide. There were two separate camps, one marked by a dirty, green World War two tent and the other, by a cheap, modern looking teepee with a circle of people crowded around outside of it. The people who inhabited the war tent must have been inside.

The group was hunched around a fire in broad daylight. They looked like they were plotting something.

These pseudo Native Americans had the palest of skin, much whiter than my own. Shirtless boys and girls draped with Tarzan and Jane type animal pelts. The strange thing was that none of the pelts looked as though they had been recently torn from an animal carcass anytime in the last decade. They were perfectly cleaned, and looked like the type of thing you'd find for sale in a museum gift shop. What's more, none of the kids there looked like they'd killed an animal with their bare hands in their lives. Not to mention that there were no wild animals except for a few over fed squirrels and chipmunks anywhere around.

The pelts were haphazardly tacked to the modern clothes the kids were already wearing; canvas sneakers, tattered blue-jeans and corduroys and raggedy sundresses on some of the girls. Safety-pins and bits of duct-tape held everything in place. One girl even had a plush anime doll, one of those Japanese cartoon character things, tattered and dirty, on a string around her neck.

Behind the tee-pee and the campfire group, there was a sight that made me uncomfortable, to say the least. A large wooden crucifix was mounted, pegged up in the ground. I didn't care much about religion, but I knew what this was for. Were they practicing sacrifices, of was this supposed to be some sort of acclamation that they were good Christians? From where I stood, I couldn't see any trace that the cross had ever been fitted with a body. There were no traces of blood or brutality to be seen. Also, the bare face of the wood had been effaced by bright colored, illegible words and markings. It was graffiti, like the sort one would find in any city.

It was even made with spray-paint, seeing that a litter of old, rusted cans had been laid to rest at the cross's base.

Were they trying to recreate a culture they didn't know or fully understand to begin with? Or was this some sort of melding of many contradictory ways of living and believing? I didn't know, but slowly approached the group.

As I walked over toward the group, a girl, or maybe, I thought, it was a boy, turned around to face me. She seemed to be the most perceptive, it felt as though she seen me standing in the distance for awhile, even though she had never turned around to face me before. But that she was waiting, expecting me to approach.

Even as I did, there was a distinct element of androgyny to her. With short, spiky, caramel brown hair, she looked like a cross between a British school boy and a woodland deer. Shirtless but with a flat chest, she had a boy's body; small, pale nipples on white-bread child's body that had browned to a state of nature with too much exposure to the sun. She wore dirty, tan colored, corduroy pants with long toes on her dirty bare-feet which poked out from the rolled up cuffs of the already too big, baggy pants. A distressed leather belt cinched up the pants around her tiny waist. Her hands, while still incredibly dirt rimmed and covered in grime, especially around her ragged, chewed fingernails, were the most feminine thing about her, and really what gave her away if indeed, she was hiding that fact.

They were tiny, delicate and ribbed with lines made from work and pain of having others depend on you, taking care of them, and losing them...when you don't care for them just right, or when time takes its course. Her blue eyes, heavy with darkness, made this girl, no older than eight years old in stature, look by far, the oldest and wisest of the group. I assumed that she was the leader. A very old person looked out of those eyes and as wise as those eyes looked, they also had the frightening quality of defeat, as if there was nothing left to lose, and Hell waited on the horizon, inevitable, and, for someone who'd spent eternity waiting in dread of it, a relief.

She paused, and straightened a bright blue, dyed feather which was tied to a black shoelace and wrapped, multiple times, around her head, a tribal headpiece of modernity. She approached me defensively, her sad hands placed firmly on her hips.

"I heard you waiting back there, in the bushes. Are you spying on us? Who sent you?" she asked.

"Uh...no one... I..." I started, but her torrent of questions didn't stop.

"Did those fascists send you to spy on us?" she barked, and pointed over to the military inspired tent.

"No. I came from the America playground. My name's

Mac. I've just been walking around this whole place. Seein' what's goin' on here."

"It's a pretty dangerous time to be "just explorin'" Mac. You see, come, sit down," she said and led me over to a log not far from the circle around the fire.

"...You see," she continued, "we're in the middle of a war, a war that has gone on for centuries."

"What, like the cowboys and the Indians?"

She smirked, like a cynical old man, "Surely, you my friend, are but jesting?"

"Huh?" I managed to articulate.

"Everyone knows those things are trifles, mere fairy tales made for the enjoyment of children. There were no such people. I should know, I've been here since the beginning of time."

"But what about your, tee-pee, your feathers and stuff, that's just like what the Indians wore?"

"I'm afraid that either you're mistaken or your histories are misinformed. You see, my people and I, we were the first living beings to inhabit this Earth."

"So...you mean your ancestors were Indians?"

"Not at all."

"You're saying that you've always been here, you, with your spray-paint and sneakers, have always been here, on this land? How, exactly, long is *always*? Because I can't imagine you've been here more than a week!"

"We've been here for over five thousand years. I see that it displeases you to find that you were born from a past you never heard of. It is not uncommon. Most people will believe in the most horrific things just as long as they've been prepared and conditioned for them. Like that awful Hell nonsense...

Anyway, my name is Chance. And these people, my people, the Savages, have bee here forever, like I said. The history books just prefer to leave us out, because of our rather...how do I say it...antagonistic actions?"

"So you've been around *forever?* Like, before Jesus?" I asked.

"Ugh..." sighed Chance, "more fairytales... Don't they teach you anything in that "real world" of yours?"

"But...but you have a huge crucifix..."

"That is not a crucifix! That is our tree of knowledge. It's how we know everything about everything. It tells us what we must do next. We were meant to fight with the fascists. They too, have been here forever. We will be defeated of course, we know this, but we must keep fighting..."

"Hah! The "tree of knowledge"! That's from the Bible! Admit it, you know it, you're just a..."

"Where," she sighed, as if explaining such obvious things to a moron like me was the most tedious chore, "do you think they got it from?"

"You're saying the writers of the Bible, got the idea for the tree of knowledge, from you, from that spray-painted stump?" I shouted, standing up and pointing to the cross.

"Yes. And please, sit back down, there's no need to shout."

"And why must you keep fighting? Why can't you just declare peace already, if you claim to have been fighting this war for thousands of years and know that you're going to lose?"

"I knew you'd ask that. The fascists, they are destined to become great heroes. They will make those history books which are so ill-informed, and will be renowned even longer than we Savages will exist in the future. Their adventures will be sung in the works of poets for the forever that's to come. We will all die, it's true, but it is not our purpose to be cherished in the minds of future generations. No, it is our purpose, however, to fight them with all our might, to provoke a great and powerful legacy from those thoughtless buffoons, and to lose our lives in the process. They, of course, do not know these things. They, of course, will think they've won because they're stronger than us... That maybe be so, but they, for all their strength will never know that the stars have determined that they will leave behind a great legacy, but also a great and tragic demise."

"Huh," I scoffed, still very skeptical of all this, "seems like there's more "greatness" around than alla you know how to deal with."

"On the contrary," beamed Chance, "and perhaps it would behoove you to focus on your own path of greatness. Perhaps it would give purpose to your wandering."

Then, there was the sound of guns in the distance, bullets dancing loudly like baby rattles on speed. The "fascists", as Chance had called them, were crouching behind bushes and shooting at us with frightening machine guns that were dripping with garlands of bullet shells. They had green suits and army hats with stickers of Buddha on the front. Great, I thought, another group of greedy, destiny driven people who worshipped things they didn't know anything about.

Chance grabbed me and dragged me behind a tree. I figured that it was only a matter of time before they shot right through the tree trunk and killed us.

"Yer gonna tell me you saw that comin'?" I gasped with disbelief.

"Of course. But like I told you, we already know we're going to lose."

10.

If landmines were people, they'd probably be neglected orphans. When they go off, they really go. It's like they know that there is nothing for them to lose, but the louder they fall the more people will know that they've always been around, and boy aren't they sorry they never noticed before!

The ground splintered next to me as one of the savage gems themselves ripped through the earth. I covered my ears and hated how helpless I felt and how accustomed I was getting to the feeling. All around me there were silent explosions. In my head I heard no noise, although there was noise all around, I heard nothing and saw great acts of violence flying in slow motion like the steps of a beautiful dance.

One of the savages took a bow and arrow, not one of those pathetic little tree branch whittled numbers, but a real modern looking god of a bow. Noiseless, as it peaked perfectly in its steel and wire shell, springing like hate's mousetrap. At the landing, the arrow dove and then attacked its' target. A sour-faced, green clad soldier fell to his knees. And then finally, face down in nameless shame, into the dirt and the green grass. He adapted to it immediately. The earth took him. It seemed to swallow him right up, as his fellow "fascists" stampeded over his body, trampling him. What was he to them? Nothing, as a foot fell to the back of his head that showed no face. A pair of black, combat boots to once pliable knees crushed his insolent bones that broke so easily under their tremulous feet.

It was harder to tell the sex of the fallen bodies on their side as it had been to identify Chance as a girl. Not only that, but there seemed to be no distinguishing features. Either they didn't exist or they had purposefully tried to erase all traces of individuals. When one fell, another, with skin just as white as the first, and eyes just as blue, replaced them.

I saw so much in what was no more than a few seconds time. I saw lives fall, people cut down at the knees like contemplative cedars. They fought each other, but they did not fight death. This war, as Chance had said, had been going on for thousands of years. Did they no longer think about why they did what they did? Had there been so much anger, upon anger for so long that there was no want of compromise? Or was this seemingly senseless slaughter really an inspiration for a legacy and heroic deeds to come? Was it truly inevitable?

I sat there, totally contemplating human existence,

when Chance pulled me by the arm and tried to drag me out onto the open battleground. Sure she was small, but, man, girls can pull when provoked by thoughts of inevitable doom!

"The hell are you doin' girl? I'm not goin' out there! No way!"

"You must," she grunted, as calmly as possible for someone dragging the last sane kid, about three times her weight by whatever she could grab a hold of.

"Uh uh. Just because you believe in this dyin' fer things we don't really want cuz' it's gona happen anyway…that shit ain't for me! I'm not gonna be nobody's sacrifice. Die cuz' you want me to? No thank you!"

We went that way, arguing in perfect harmony with each other and with the battle field we wove in and around. She dragged me and I resisted, yanking her away, clawing at her sad hands, anything I could do to break free and run, about a mile away, in any direction these people weren't. I'd hop over a soldier laying on the ground, wounded, firing a rattle of shells from his machine gun and trying to roll out of enemy's range. Chance, meanwhile, was dodging and pulling me under the arches of bows and guns made by a solid line of her people aiming their weapons at ninety degree angles. It looked effortless the way we moved, like we had both been choreographed in past lives or some bullshit, to do so. If I had been anyone else watching us, I would have thought that movements that perfect and horrific could only be engineered in dreams or Broadway musicals.

"Get this straight," she shouted as we darted behind some tall metal drums and crouched until she saw a temporary cease fire, "I don't want you dead and that's not what's going to happen to you alright? Not here. And not by my hand, you won't die."

"And I'm supposed to believe all this because a wooden post told you? Why should I do that?"

"Because you will, it's inevitable."

Then, she pushed me and quite off guard, and I found myself caught in between a boy with a rifle and a line of savages, all tied together with a rope nailed into the ground on both sides. One of them had managed to get out a pocket knife and cut the rope, they were in the process of wriggling free, when a small boy from the other camp had spotted them and decided to shoot them before they could escape. Not only escape, but reach a gun that had fallen just outside of their reach. The young fascist looked as though killing one more person, me, wouldn't hurt his chances of surviving just long enough to kill some more savages. He cocked his gun to aim.

All this happened in a second. You wouldn't believe how many people will say, "why didn't you just run, or move out of the way?" whenever you tell them a story in which you find yourself in a position where you're surrounded by "hostile forces on both sides", as some great philosopher, I can't remember who, once said. People who have the audacity to ask such a question are usually the ones who cringe at the idea that you can't save yourself. They hate feeling helpless, and think there must always be some other option. But helpless is the way you feel when you're the diversion set between a fighting mountain lion and bear.

People think if the world you're in is of your own creation, you'll always be able to control it. But creations have a habit of wanting control and power of their own, even at the expense of their creator. Anyone who either believes in god or has parents will know that there is more resentment from one's creations than gratitude.

What happened next you might not believe, but another soldier from the fascist side ran at me and knocked me out of the way. He then got on one knee, aimed his rifle and shot every one of the escaping savages. My jaw dropped. I didn't know whether to be traumatized at his mass slaughter or eternally grateful to him that I hadn't died. I heard his people, the ones who had seen the event, cheer and keep on shooting. He then railed on his fellow soldier,

"Never, I repeat Never, shoot an innocent bystander! Do you hear me?"

"Yes sir," the poor kid nodded.

"We're only here to kill the enemy. Don't make us into monsters," he said and then ran off.

I stood there, very confused. Weren't they monsters already? They had killed all those people. In their own minds they were heroes and their people would go on to celebrate them as heroes. But I didn't know what to think.

Was one life saved, one good deed, really enough to make him "good", (whatever that meant anymore)? Or was it just easier to identify one group as evil, and then everything that one of them does is seen collectively and used as more ammunition for hatred? Perhaps it was nothing more than my difference in appearance from the savages that was the reason for my life being saved.

I looked behind me to see if Chance was there. If she had known that the fascist would save me, was it true that there was an inevitable destiny? If she hadn't pushed me into there path, would he have intervened on my behalf? I couldn't tell if this event proved her right or proved that she was choosing to create the future she wanted to see. When I looked for her however, I saw her, in the distance, curled up like an infant waiting to be born, under the graffiti covered cross that the savages called the Tree of Life. Her fetal position expressed no anguish. Her eyes were not visible since her head was tucked into her chest and the hands that had once looked so sad and wearied with the past actions and wisdoms, curled around her head, as if protecting a sacred jewel inside her skull. This was a jewel of grand design.

The stillness was definitive enough for me to know it wasn't temporary. Chance died protecting her dream of an unfortunate, predestined future which she took solace in because it gave her the power of knowing what was to come. What was there to fear if you knew that all the terrible things you would do and experience were a sacrifice necessary to the betterment of your species? Even in death, her posture protected the idea she lived and for. Despite her brutality and ugliness, Chance was similar to Lyddie in that way. They were people in constant motion, speeding toward a brutal and beautiful light of their own making.

11.

They were visible from far away. I could tell they weren't
going to stop. Packs of them, disorganized mobs, rushing
and screaming, separate but together. Faceless masses
waving guns and other weapons. Child faces, stained with
youth, were also streaked with blood and dirt and held
intensities far greater than their understanding. They
were beautiful in their modern, primitive glory. They were
beautiful in a violent, terrifying way. The sort that human
violence you could identify with as something deep, yet
forbidden inside most of us. I didn't know whether to hate
or admire them for their blind passion. I don't suppose it
would have mattered. Like a herd of stampeding gazelle,
they just did what they did.

All of them were ready to draw blood. I couldn't tell who
they were angry at but they were rushing in the direction of
the already warring fascists and savages. The groups were
all in front of me, the kids from the playground of the
overseer, ones from the American playground and the prison
ground, all raging toward us like an angry white light.

I could feel them closing in on me. Although there was a torrent of unidentifiable rage tunneling straight for me and I felt strangely detached. I didn't know if it had something to do with being desensitized from all the warring going on at the savage playground, but I knew that all this had nothing to do with me. I certainly felt powerless, that hadn't changed. But, all my watching throughout that long day, which held days in itself and seemed to last a lifetime, had taught me nothing if not that people wanted to die, were happy to martyr themselves, in order to prove that everything they believed in was real. Their ideals were what was killing them, but they wouldn't get rid of them. Ideals are the parents of orphans. They're the captors that never stop loving their captives and us captives, we're the children that never want to be free.

Then, far in the distance, I saw Christian. First I thought he was standing still, alone and unaware of the hostility surrounding him. But I realized he was part of the ensuing mob. He had stayed, no doubt, in the overseer's playground with Calli, too afraid to venture forth on his own. I assumed even then, that if he were part of any playground's army, he was following Calli to the brink of destruction.

Strangely enough, I didn't see her face in the crowd, no at the head, where Christian was, nor any place throughout. My little brother was still silent. I heard none of the yells and shrieks of his peers, but there was a conviction in his face, the firm anger in which his eyes were set, that frightened me and made me regret ever having taken him to this place.

It had affected him in ways I couldn't have imagined. I thought that he could look around observe objectively, like I did, take what he liked and leave the rest. That didn't happen. He had really been transformed. Or, maybe some lonely, lost part of him had been waiting, always, for something like Orphan Park, to give him something to believe in enough to kill and to die for. Like all the other kids here, he had waited all his life to release his anger, to find something worth fighting for, killing for and dying for.

He was at the head of the group, clad in armor that looked like the remnants of a Greek play. Pieces of shining silver plates hung from their chests and skirted their slender children's bodies. Christian was the leader of all of them! I couldn't believe it. Christian, just eight years old, with his firm set eyes and no hint of his own voice, was leading an army.

At the end of the pack, was a small, blonde haired girl. She was dragging something behind her on a rope. I couldn't tell what it was from afar, but as the army approached, screaming and charging, I identified the object being dragged on the rope. It was a human head. The bloodied stump, decapitated from its' body, looked like a lifeless pet that had been loved to death. The hair was brown and the face was not that of a very young child but that of a young adult. It was Calli. It was such a frightening sight since at afar, it seemed like such an innocent sight, nothing more than a little girl dragging a wooden pony or doll. And despite her kindness, her stability and maturity, she too had come to just as tragic an end as all the rest of them. The most unfortunate thing was that she had no story to go along with her death. No tragic or heroic demise that would be remembered and retold as a lesson for future generations. Even the way her head was treated, dragged on the ground through the dirt, showed that her type of power couldn't last, that she too would be brought down and made a mockery of by the people who had once worshipped and depended on her.

The group Christian was leading found its' rage met with that of another army. The prison-ground army headed them face on and I could see Lily was at the head. Amir was no where in sight. It seemed that he too had been overthrown by those he had controlled for so long. She was in control at last, like she had wanted and even thought was prophesized as her future. She thought she was setting those people free, but really she had just usurped Amir as the leader. She was screaming and waving a hatchet and drawing the anger inside of them up, so that she could wage war on everything and everyone who could take her newly found power away from her.

The two of them, Lyddie and Christian and their respective armies, were running towards each other on the battle field. But it was all about them. Their personal angers of their pasts were driving them. For Lyddie, it was her memories of a murderous and tyrannical father who had killed her mother and kept her prisoner. For Christian, it was the silence that he wanted to break, his inability to control anything in his life, from being neglected by his drug addicted mother to being given up for adoption. No matter what he did, he just couldn't get her attention. Sure, sometimes she might have smiled affectionately through a drug induced haze, but it never lasted. He had never been able to control her love and being a kid, he could never control where he lived or which stranger his life would be entrusted to next. Battle was something both he any Lyddie could control. Although one of them was sure to lose.

Not that it made any sense. Not really. Whatever the supposed conflict between the two playgrounds was severely less important to their two leaders than their need to prove their separate powers. But closer and closer they got, and I was standing separate, off to the side, watching the soon to be destruction of my lover or my brother.

Then, he struck her. His long, scythe-like sword gouged her stomach. Her stomach, that I had kissed so often that night when we were hidden from the world. My mouth fell open in horror. My brother, that was my brother that did this to her, I thought, as she fell and crumpled onto the ground. I knew she was dead. I also knew that that fact did nothing if not fuel the hate and vengeance of her people who fought even harder for her effort, and crushed her lifeless body with their trampling feet.

How could I take Christian home after what had just happened? Talk to him about girls I liked and teachers who were nasty? How could I bring him back to Mamma Jewell and let her call him her baby? Was he an innocent still? Was this all my fault for introducing him to such a cruel world? Or did he know better than to kill? Was there anything else he could've done besides kill or be killed? Can one bad deed wipe out a lifetime of good ones? Can his cruelty in that moment ever be lessened by the hurt and learned hatred of his past?

I still haven't found the answers to these questions. I've heard however, that no one ever thinks of themselves as a bad person. No matter what you've done, you always have a reason for it, so it all makes sense to you. But the look on Christian's face looked sobered. He dropped the scythe and the hoards of children in the army he once lead, rushed in front of him continuing to fight the remaining Babylonians. He stopped moving and they passed him by.

What was I supposed to do? I thought. There was the girl, with whom I had loved, if only for the momentary happiness she gave me. But it was no less strong a love for that. In my mind I had lived many lives with her, and truthfully, I do still.

In these fantasies I had imagined us as separate from this world, in a place where turmoil was less constant. In those dreams I introduced her to my foster mother and we dated, went to college together and then, later I proposed. It was on a winter morning when we woke up next to each other, after spending a night shivering half naked and holding each other while we slept on our little love stained mattress in a shitty, starter apartment. When she heard the news, she would have jumped up and down on the bed wearing only her panties and a camisole. She was beautiful, but my thoughts at her near nakedness then, were of nothing but a child-like endearment of her to me.

She was a teacher, and I, with my talents for observation was a photographer and we took vacations into strange and wild places. I took pictures there and sent them to nature magazines. But all our adventures took us home to a safe place where we grew old and watched the travels and explorations of our children and consoled them that what they did meant something to us, that every day of their lives led to a greater understanding of a beautiful world and not just closer to their deaths and the deaths of the parasitic species they belonged to.

I dreamed of the repetitive, banal life that so many try to escape. Most people want to escape into excitement at any cost. I knew better. Young men who leapt at the chance of war, they are never satisfied. Either they don't recognize their mistake until it's too late, or they live forever in what is considered the "calm after the storm". It is a purgatory of the mind, the closest thing to heaven or hell, and the cruelest. When young men return from war their faces show that they have aged a great deal. There is emptiness behind their eyes. Nothing can excite them like the horrible things they've seen. As much as the soldiers, the ones who make it at all, try to block out all the death they've seen and all the hurt it has caused, somewhere in the back of their minds, they are traumatized with excitement. The adrenaline rush is so great that no other stimulus in life can ever live up to it. And when they go home, they stare off, seemingly hollow but internally anxious, waiting for their lives to begin again.

In my fantasies, I dreamt of a place where Lyddie and I put those needs to rest and took solace in the love we found in each other. But, in reality, things were not that way. She was gone, and no revenge I could ever take upon Christian, nor shunning of him, could bring her back or ever make him fully understand what he had taken from me. So I made a decision.

I made a decision and it started me running. It started me feeling like I hadn't felt in days, like I had a purpose. So many times I had roamed across a violent land and felt nothing. Or if I felt anything, there was nothing I could do to change it, so I would care for nothing but to move on and out of fear, save my own life. I could not say, nor can I now, with any certainty, that I am a good human being, but from what I have witnessed in my lifetime, I am one with strange and powerful loyalties.

I ran past the army that had left my brother behind and when I reached him, I grabbed his hand, which was cold, but because of the distance, had been spared any blood from the life he had just taken. He looked up at me, seeming surprised and a little scared that I had seen him like this, in his anger and what he done. And his eyes looked at me as if to ask how I could still love him and take his hand.

I did. I pulled him by the arm, as I had when we were arriving at the park, and ran, over the hill, through the red sunset that bled, slowly over the belly of the hill, covering it. We ran all the way home. Christian looked at me as if to say,

"What are we doing?"

We weren't cowards. I kept telling myself that we weren't cowards as we ran, our limbs flouncing in different directions, we were like sparklers lit on the fourth of July, burning brightly. If not forever, just for now, and that, that would be enough. We were just more short lived things of summer days. All summer things burn up eventually. There is just too much passion, to much love to much anger, to be contained forever.

Like the feet of children running through your kitchen in the palpable heat of a summer's day, streaming, bustling, noisily, across screened in porches and out into turmoil. We knew what we were doing. And like I said, we weren't cowards. We were going to face the park and all the orphans who had brought it to the peak of its destruction. We were going back. But we needed to get something first.

"Whatcha doin' comin' home so late? Dontcha know it's nearly eight o'clock?" Mamma Jewell yelled out the window at us. She seemed more tired and weary of life than angry. We made our way to the garage as I said,

"Don't worry Momma, we'll be back before ten. We just gotta go back an' finish somethin'.'"

"Be back by ten he says!" she huffed, pretending to sound indignant, but I couldn't help but detect a certain level of pride in her voice that I had found something that I wanted enough to give me that kind of stubbornness, to give me the "fight" as they call it, the spirit, the will, to go against the routine of "supposed to". She herself wished she could break it, but her routine held the lives of me, Christian and the babies in the balance, so she kept at it, out of love you could say.

"Yeah, you better be! Its school t'morrow and I won't have you boys missin' any more of it!" she said.

We nodded to pacify her. But we had a more important mission ahead of us than the banality of the routine she lived in. Mamma Jewell had been my legal guardian for about as long as I could remember. But for all her kindness, there was no choice in her possessing me nor was I destined from birth to be hers. I saw her as my mother no more than I did my biological mother. Neither, I could picture, her putting down her Schnapps and coffee and armfuls of other foster kids to run down a battle field fueled by me and the thought of my love.

Within the past day I had seen people dying for ideas. Ideas that were like drugs to them, which gave them a sense of understanding they could not live without. But in reality, it was the power of knowing that so many, like

Lyddie and Chance, craved. They claimed to believe in predestined and inevitable things, but really, it was their choices, (like when Chance pushed me in front of the soldiers), that made their beliefs come true and reinforced them further.

We found a ladder in the garage. Covered in cobwebs, we delicately marveled at the unused relic with our touch. Dusty and wooden, with wobbly matching steps, it was as magnificent as an ancient, dilapidated forest. It was almost like a tree itself.

"Here," I said to Christian, "you carry this end and we'll take it back there."

He looked alarmed, as if scared to go back to the park. He was afraid to meet the person he had transformed into after belonging to a society like the ones in the park. Being the leader, believing in your people and their ways and having them believe in him.

I took the head of the ladder, while Christian took the short wobbly wooden legs. Together we shuffled and guided the ladder down the cracked sidewalk and over the hill back to the park we had abandoned not long ago. But unlike our own parents, Christian and I were coming back. We were going back to become the adults we had always needed in our own lives. I had a plan, which came from a choice and that choice was mine, my own. I would become the guardian of all the orphans in the park, even if they didn't care or appreciate it. I felt I had to take action.

When we got there, we carried the ladder into the center

of the field. I didn't have to explain to Christian what it was for. You can call that fate, as if he understood the purpose, a mutual understanding, or you can call it trust, which is what I prefer to leave it at. But whatever the reason, he followed me and then, right then like no other time I had experienced before, I was certain. Certain of what I must do and why, despite how impossible it seemed.

Often, when people don't know the answer to something, "why am I here?" etcetera, you find them always looking up. Most often it's because they are looking to god to drop down a diagnosis quicker and more certain than figuring out an individual answer for themselves, which could take a lifetime and still have the possibility of leaving you with nothing. I was looking up to. But this time, it was to something I could control, although I can't say just how I knew it would work and perhaps that, in itself is a testament to a kind of faith.

The fighting continued all around us, but we could not be swayed. Christian held the ladder firmly to the ground and must have been immovable because none of the fighters came within a circle of our private mission. They fought around us, physically unaware of our presence but sensing a need for distance from the spot we stood in as if it was encircled by an enchantment.

So I began climbing. The motion was new to me, the climbing, but there was a ritual to it that felt as though I had been doing it all of my life. Going up and up, always reaching for a greater thing always wanting to get higher.

But when I got to the clouds, I found that they were extremely physical. They look, from the ground, transparent and without physical substance. In reality, they were more like a platform masked with wisps of fog and smoke, camouflaging the rigidity of air. The fireless smoke rings wrapped around me, after I had climbed off the ladder. In their embrace I felt peacefully trapped. It is a feeling of contradiction, the likes of which I cannot quite explain, but it might help me to compare it to the feeling of destiny. There is no doubt, you see, or uncertainty, which constantly plagues the human mind because of the powerlessness it provides. In the comforting entrapment however, there is only knowledge only worshipful devotion and conviction. Even if the destiny is restrictive or terrible, there is some sort of comfort in knowing that there is nothing you could do. But that was not the way of the real world, the one in which orphans kill orphans, and I could not stay in the comfort of that feeling.

In the clouds I felt like how the figure inside a painting must feel. You are the only solid thing in the midst of a swirling, malleable eye to which the attentions of others are drawn. This time, I would not accept the drift of the clouds, of the world surrounding me. I searched the clouds I had climbed off onto, crawling on them with my knees, pounding on them with my fists, anything. Anything I could do to force an act of nature.

And then it started, burst open like a hole in the sky. Snow started falling everywhere. As if all the anger the clouds had been bearing burst, finally, out like a resentful child. But the anger was slow, and soft and very beautiful. Maybe it was more like strength than anger, or personal identity, the distinguishing of oneself from their parent land.

I started climbing down the ladder as the snow fell, feeling triumphant although I didn't know quite yet as to why I felt so. But I was certain that the snow would stop the fighting. The cold of it, the strangeness of it occurring on a hot, murderous summer day, or the purity of it, contrasted to the angry, red sky. And as I climbed, I looked down to see if my plan had worked.

It had. Or at least, they had dropped their weapons. All of the children, the previous fighters, were looking up, watching and wondering where this "Miracle" had come from. Would they have ever believed I had created it? Would they want to believe it? They watched in awe, maybe even fear as I worked my way back to the earth. For the first time since my arrival there, they had started acting like the scared and confused children they were. Always looking up, but still never knowing. Oh the doubt! Oh the wonderful uncertainty! And of course, with that comes true chance, with that came choice.

They were taking off their shields and removing their armor. It was clear that the battle was over, that it was time to stop playing. One of the overseer playground's children, a small dirty-blond haired boy looked up at me, smirking, and said, "Hey asshole, what'd you go an' do that for? We were just startin' to have fun, you know, git to the good parts?" he added, making a forward, jabbing gesture with one of his fists in a stabbing motion.

My frustration surged. They wanted to die. They wanted to kill each other! They didn't care that I had saved them, or at least, they expressed no gratitude. I thought to myself, I should have let them kill each other. But soon, my anger subsided. My decision to save them wasn't even about them anymore at all, maybe it never was.

Christian looked at me. As usual, he said nothing. Only this time, it was just the right thing for me to say. The kids here, for a time, had known exactly what they wanted, what they believed in and what they needed to protect. Before I came here, I was a stranger to those ways, I thought myself an impartial observer. It wasn't always that I was able to open the sky by my own willing it and stop the river of death from flowing into the sea, if only for the time being. In some ways, I was always as orphan, I was always like them. I belonged in this place although I didn't know it. I had become the grownup I had always waited for. Unlike them, I didn't always know what I wanted or who I needed to protect. But I do now.

Printed in the United States
153712LV00008B/130/P